Echoes of Fate

Megan Bradish

This is a work of fiction. Names, characters, businesses, events, and incidents are products of the author's imagination. Any resemblance to actual persons, living or dead, or actual events is purely coincidental.

Printed in the United States by Amazon's Kindle Direct Publishing.

ISBN: 9798358808591

To the dreamers who never stop believing in the unbelievable. For the souls who wander through the shadows of the unknown, seeking the whispers of the universe and the secrets hidden in the starlight.

Note From The Author

I began writing this novel nearly five years ago. For a long time, I set it aside, waiting for the perfect moment to complete it. This story holds a special place in my heart, and I didn't want to rush it. The idea came to me through my own dreams. I've always believed there's more to dreams than mere imagination—they possess a deeper meaning, a hidden truth waiting to be uncovered. The intrigue of dreams, combined with my love for all things medieval and mysterious, inspired me to write this book. Over the years, I have nurtured and refined it, and it is now ready to be shared with the world. I hope you all enjoy reading it as much as I have enjoyed writing it.

Chapter 1

The rain pours down in sheets, each drop pounding viciously into the soil, creating small rivers of mud that flow relentlessly. Lightning streaks across the sky, splitting the darkness with electric brilliance, reminiscent of ancient roots pushing through the ground in a desperate search for life. In the distance, I see a cave nestled within a towering cliff, its mouth a dark void. To the side, the waves crash and moan in rhythm with the storm, their thunderous roar a counterpoint to the sky's fury.

"Ren, we need to hurry! She's coming!" a man yells over the deafening roar of the rain.

I know he's right, but a part of me wants to drop to my knees and cry until it all goes away. Exhaustion clings to me like a second skin, and my lungs burn with every ragged breath. We've been on the run for hours, traversing treacherous mountain terrain and dense underbrush that has scratched my shins raw. Twigs whip across my face, leaving stinging cuts that bleed into my eyes.

"I don't think I can!" I cry out, my voice barely audible over the storm.

"Yes, you can, love! You have to!" he replies, his grip firm as he grabs my hand and practically drags me across the sand towards the cliffside.

"We'll wait it out here," he says, inspecting the cave with a critical eye.

It's small, barely noticeable to the human eye, its entrance camouflaged by shadows. The black walls are covered with small crystals that shimmer eerily, even though there's no light to reflect. It's as if the cave itself is alive, a silent guardian protecting us from the dangers lurking in the night.

I cling to him, hugging his neck tightly. I inhale the sweet musk of his sweat-stained skin, the familiar scent calming my racing heart, and sigh deeply.

"We can't let her win. We can't let her do this to us. I need you," I whisper, my fingers trembling as I caress his face softly.

He gently cups my face in his hands and looks deep into my eyes, his gaze steady and unyielding.

"We will never be apart. We are stronger than her," he promises, his voice a soothing balm.

"But she has the weapon. She'll kill us!" I begin to sob, the weight of dread crushing my heart.

"Ren, sweetheart, I need you to trust me. We will defeat her. I promise you that."

"How?" I ask, the question a desperate plea. "She's immortal," I add, my voice barely a whisper.

"So are we," he points out, his words a lifeline.

"She at least has a weapon to kill us. We have nothing!" My voice cracks with despair.

"I know," he says, his tone resolute. "But we will find one. It's out there. And I will never stop looking. I'll search the ends of the earth, and every hidden corner. And if that doesn't work, I'll go beyond. I'll

explore every realm for a weapon to kill her once and for all. Because I am not going to lose you. I love you more than anything," he declares, his eyes blazing with determination.

His eyes flicker in the flash of lightning, and my heart bursts with love for the man holding me in his strong arms. The storm's fury seems to pale in comparison to the fire in his gaze.

I lean in closer, and he kisses me with such passion that the world around me feels like it's crumbling beneath my feet. The storm, the cave, the danger—all fade away, leaving only the two of us, bound together by an unbreakable bond.

Chapter 2

I wake with sweat trickling down my forehead, my heart still pounding from the thought of losing the man from my dream. The remnants of the dream cling to me like a shadow, the vivid imagery refusing to fade. This isn't the first time I've had a dream like this. Every time, it's with the same man, the same burning love. I have no idea who he is; I've never seen him before in my life. But there's a nagging feeling that my soul knows him intimately. I used to think I was crazy for feeling this way. Honestly, it sounds a little crazy. But now, I think of it like any other feeling—there's something to it, and it's become a part of who I am.

The dreams started when I was in my early teens. I didn't think much of them at first, dismissing them as mere fantasies. Now, at twenty-eight, they're more frequent, more persistent. They're calling out to me, but I have no idea what any of it means. It's as though the man who lives in my dreams is trying to tell me something. Something vital.

As I think back on his touch, the hair stands at attention on my arms. Usually, dreams fade from your memory over time; bits and pieces start fading. Faces blur until eventually, there's nothing left to remember. But these dreams are different. I remember every little detail, especially his face. His eyes are a deep green, like I'm looking into a dark, mysterious forest. His jaw is sharp, adorned with dark brown stubble that gives him a rugged charm. His lips are soft, full, and inviting. He's tall with a strong, solid build, his muscles bulging and moving under his shirt. Tattoos creep down his arms and peek through the sleeves, intricate designs that tell untold stories.

And when I wake, I can still feel his touch. His arms wrapped around my small frame, the heat from his skin coursing through my body. And his lips brushing softly against mine, leaving a lingering warmth.

Of all the times I have fallen in love, I have never felt a love as strong as I do with this man. I never knew I had that kind of love inside of me. Not until the dreams started. In fact, I don't think it's humanly possible to feel so intensely. It's like an ember has ignited in my entire soul.

Now it's burning hot, and I don't know if there's a chance of ever meeting him. Let's face it, he probably doesn't even exist. But despite that, the more I think of this man, the emptier I feel. Like a deep void has filled my entire being. Like a whole part of me is missing.

I feel lost, like I don't really fit in the world, or with the people in it. I've always felt that way, from the time I was a small child. I've never had many friends; I just could never seem to make them no matter how badly I wanted to or how hard I tried. Part of the problem might be that no one seems to really hear me. Trying to join in on conversations has always been a chore. Any time I've ever tried, everyone talks over me, like I'm not even in the room. It's truly exhausting and lonely.

But when I'm asleep, I've never felt more alive. I know that these dreams are what keep me going. And I know I have to find the life I've always dreamed about. Am I even positive it exists? Not entirely, but I feel like it has to... somewhere.

The sun is peeking brightly through my window, so I flick on my phone to check the time. Eight o'clock. I really could have gone for a few more hours of a nice, deep sleep. Actually, I could stay in bed all day with no complaints. With depression, and the fact that my dreams, or more so, the reality of my dreams seeming so far away, makes me feel... weird. It's the only way I know how to describe it.

Just as I'm drifting back to sleep, I hear a knock at my front door. My eyes pop open, and I sigh, knowing who it probably is. I grumble as I get out of bed and make my way down the hallway. The hardwood floor is cool against my bare feet, a stark contrast to the warmth of my bed. As I get closer to the kitchen, I see Sheila, my childhood best friend, at the door, bright-eyed and smiling, waving excitedly through the small window.

"Hey, Sheil," I say as I open the door for her.

"Hi, girl!" she says, pushing her way through and plopping down on the kitchen chair with the ease of someone who has done it a thousand times.

I sit down next to her, massaging my fingers. They've been bothering me since the dreams started. They tingle, sometimes hurt, and sometimes feel like they're going to explode all at the same time.

Sheila eyes me up, concern crossing her face. "You look tired," she points out.

"Well, yeah. I just crawled out of bed," I say, hoping she will let it go.

"No," she shakes her head. "It's more than that. You look stressed, or maybe sad."

I sigh in defeat. "You've always been able to see right through me."

"We've been best friends since we were kids. I know you, Ren."

Ren. The man in my dreams calls me that too. But why shouldn't he? Everyone else in my life calls me Ren, instead of Serenity. It's only logical that I would incorporate that into my dreams.

I begin to think of the most recent dream. The terror, the love. What did it all mean?

Embarrassed by my own thoughts, I look down at my hands again, my face turning beet red. Maybe I am crazy. Maybe I'm actually losing my mind, having some kind of psychotic break, and this is how it presents itself to me. But I feel it. And my soul feels like it's on fire.

"Um, hello. Earth to Ren," Sheila says as she waves her hand in front of my face.

"Sorry," I say. "I had the dream again."

Sheila looks at me with pity. "You know they're just dreams, right?" she asks in a soft voice.

No, as a matter of fact. I don't know that they're just dreams. I'm not sure of anything anymore. But I couldn't tell Sheila that. Knowing her, she'd have me hauled off to an institution somewhere.

"Of course, I know it's just a dream," I say.

"So, what's the matter? Why do they affect you the way that they do?"

I begin to feel defensive as anger rises to a boil in my blood. "I don't know, Sheila. Why do nightmares affect you? Is there something wrong with you too?"

Immediately regretting my outburst, I look away, trying to hold back the tears that are threatening to fall. I just need someone to talk to. But I know if I do talk about it, everyone would just think I'm crazy. Because I know it sounds like I'm losing it.

"Ren, I'm sorry. I didn't mean to upset you," Sheila says as she stares at me cautiously.

"Me too," I sigh. "I'm just stressed lately. Can you forgive me?"

Sheila smiles. "There's nothing to forgive," she says as she stands, walking over to the coffee pot. "Now, how about some coffee?"

Chapter 3

Sheila stayed for a couple more hours as we drank our coffee and gossiped about everything we could think of. The rich aroma of freshly brewed coffee filled the air, mingling with the scent of cinnamon from the homemade muffins Sheila had brought. We laughed until our stomachs hurt, tears of joy rolling down our cheeks. The sound of our laughter echoed through the cozy kitchen, a symphony of happiness that I cherished deeply. I've always loved it when we could talk and laugh like that. It always came so easily to us, no matter how long we went without seeing each other. We could fall right back into the same routine as if no time had passed at all, our bond as strong as ever.

Although Sheila doesn't understand everything about me, I would be lost without her. Her unwavering support and infectious enthusiasm are like a lifeline in my often turbulent life. I want to tell her everything, right down to how deeply I feel for the man I don't even know exists. But I know it would be impossible for Sheila to understand. I can hardly grasp it myself, so I can't expect others to understand.

After Sheila leaves, I decide to do some work in my garden. It's my happy place, a sanctuary where

I can lose myself in the soothing rhythm of nature. I feel at peace tending to my plants, feeling the cool soil beneath my hands, the earthy scent grounding me. There's just something about knowing you're needed. In this case, it's my garden. The plants rely on me to water them and pick off their dead leaves so they can thrive, their vibrant colors a testament to my care.

The view behind my small stone cottage is breathtaking. Though I've lived here since the day I moved out of my mother's house at the age of eighteen, I still can't get over how beautiful the view is. A vast meadow stretches as far as the eye can see, a sea of green dotted with wildflowers that sway gently in the breeze. A tall oak tree stands proud in the middle of the field, its branches sprawling out in every direction like a giant umbrella. In the evening, as the sun begins to sink low in the sky, it peeks out through the tree's branches, casting a golden glow that makes the whole scene look like a painting.

The front yard is equally beautiful. Shrubs border it, completely isolating my house from the outside world, creating a private haven. The garden bed sits off to the side with big, low-hanging willow trees nearby, their branches swaying lazily in the breeze, casting dappled shadows on the ground. On the other side is a small patio with a fireplace, the perfect spot for cozy evenings. A stone walkway leads from the gate up to the cottage, flowers lining up in rows on either side, their blossoms adding a splash of color. If I never had to leave my small sanctuary again, I wouldn't mind one bit.

After caring for the plants, I change my clothes, opting for a comfortable yet stylish outfit. I slap on a little makeup, just enough to make me feel put together, and head into town. It's a small town in the state of Maine, quaint and quiet, with charming old-fashioned buildings lining the streets. The town has one grocery store, a small bar where all the fishermen gather after a long day of work, which is also my place of employment. Other than that, there's a small bakery that fills the air with the sweet smell of fresh bread, and a cozy bookstore that feels like stepping back in time. That's it. If you need anything besides beer and food, you'd have to go to the next town over. But I like it that way, not having many people around. I've never been much of a people person. Most that I encounter are miserable, judgmental, and downright rude.

I get to the bar to pick up my check before heading to the grocery store. The bar is dimly lit, with wooden tables and chairs that have seen better days, but it has a certain charm. Once done there, I head back home and turn on the evening news. As I flick through the channels, there's nothing on but reports of rapes, murders, and politics. I roll my eyes as I turn off the TV, throwing the remote down in frustration. Living in a world so full of scum and violence drains me more often than not, and I can't help but feel like I don't belong here. Like I really belong someplace else. And I know it all stems back to the dreams that I have. I wish more than anything I could shake this feeling so I could stop living a half-life, but I can't.

My phone pings with a message, snapping me from my thoughts. I flick it on, to see it's from my mom.

Hi, sweety! Don't forget, dinner at my house tomorrow. 5 O'clock.

I feel dread in the pit of my stomach. Though, I love my mom more than life itself, these dinners always consist of her friends asking me every kind of personal question you can think of. But I suck it up and text her back.

I'll be there. Have to work, so I can't stay long.
With that, I set my phone down and close my eyes.

Chapter 4

I look at myself in the mirror, ensuring that everything is just so. Mother insists on it. My brown eyes glimmer softly as the afternoon sun peeks through the window, casting a warm glow on my face. My eyebrows are arched and shaped perfectly, and my full, dark hair is tied up in a stylish bun. A few rebellious strands hang loose, flowing over my face. I quickly tuck them away and suck in a deep breath, steadying myself for the task ahead.

It is almost time to welcome the new knights to Duix. Sir Edmond, my uncle, is in charge of finding and training the new recruits. The plague of 1473 had decimated our ranks, killing more than half of our men. It was a devastating time for the realm. I can still see the dead bodies, lying scattered over the castle grounds and the surrounding villages. Men, women, and children alike succumbed to a brutal end. Every time I close my eyes, the visions of those terrifying days still haunt me.

Eventually, life began to return to normal. The plague dissipated, and we tried to move on as though it had all been a terrible nightmare. Now, Duix is in desperate need of more knights. There's always a threat looming in the shadows, and we never know when we might need to fight. Because of that, we must always be ready.

The door to my chamber flings open. "Serenity, are you ready?" Mother asks with a disapproving look.

Mother Celest is a cruel and wicked woman. She cares nothing for the people of Duix, only for her power and fortune. She especially despises the lower-class citizens and would hang anyone who crossed her or looked at her in a way she deemed unfit. No trials, no understanding—just immediate death. Celest's favorite execution method is beheading, placing the heads on pikes for all to see. It's her friendly reminder to the people of who she is and what she's capable of. Everyone fears her, but I fear her the most. Though I am her daughter, Celest has never treated me like one. Since childhood, she has called me hateful names and hit me if I ever stepped out of line. Once, she even threw me in the cells for nothing more than being late to dinner.

As the years went on, my fear of her has been replaced with anger and a thirst for vengeance. I need to get away from this woman, but being a princess, it isn't easy to just walk away.

"Yes, mother," I answer as I stand.

"Smooth out your dress, for heaven's sake. You look a mess," Celest says, walking over to me and eyeing me up and down.

"You must always look your very best. You're to be the next queen of Duix," she adds.

I roll my eyes. "You're immortal, mother. Unfortunately, you'll never die. Therefore, I'll never be queen."

Celest's eyes fill with rage as she slaps me hard across the face. "Listen here, you little wench. Just because you're my daughter doesn't mean I won't have you executed for treason," she says, turning away. "Now come. We have three hundred knights to welcome. This will take a while."

I follow her out the door, cursing under my breath, wishing for once in my mother's miserable life that she wasn't immortal.

The knights are in the courtyard, standing proud and tall in one long, perfectly straight line. Mother and I welcome them all, one by one, for what feels like most of the day. The men seem to be very nice and upstanding gentlemen. Uncle would never settle for anything less. He always says that the knights aren't only to protect the realm, but also the women of the castle. If they were to be around us and protecting us, they couldn't be anything less than perfect gentlemen.

We're at the end of the long row of knights, with only one left to welcome.

"Sir Vincent Atticus of House Brelin," Uncle introduces.

"Serenity," I say, introducing myself.

"Princess Serenity," mother corrects.

The knight slowly slips off his helmet, revealing his perfectly chiseled face. His green eyes are fierce and bold, his thick brown hair tousled from the helmet.

My heart leaps into my chest, and my knees weaken, a small gasp escaping my lips. This man looks like a god. I've never seen a more gorgeous man in my entire life.

A fire sparks deep within my soul as he gently clasps my hand, kissing it softly.

"It's a pleasure, your highness," he says in a low, resonant tone.

If I'm not mistaken, he looks exactly as I feel. The fire burning in his eyes as he looks at me has my nerves jumping in my skin.

"Yes..." is all I can manage to say, for I'm far too nervous to say more. He seems to notice, for he gives me a devilish grin.

I've been too caught up with the sight of our new knight to notice mother's reaction until he introduces himself to her. She looks pale and frightened, as if she had just seen a ghost. Confusion sets in as I search her face. I've never seen mother afraid of anything in her entire life. She has never been afraid of anything. People were afraid of her, not the other way around. So, what had her so spooked?

I look back to Vincent. He doesn't seem to notice mother's reaction to him, for he's too busy staring at me. He can't seem to take his eyes away from mine, even as he speaks to mother. Even though he is addressing his queen, his eyes stay locked on mine. My stomach flips as my face burns hot. I can't look away; it's as though something is drawing us together with an irresistible force.

"Serenity, come," mother says as she drags me away.

I eye her warily as we head back to the castle. I can't help but look back one more time at Sir Vincent as he stares after me.

Once we reach the steps, mother turns to face me. "Stay away from him, Serenity," she warns, her frightened look quickly turning to anger.

"W-why, mother?" I ask, startled by her harsh tone. I should be used to it by now, but I still get shocked by the little things mother manages to throw herself into a tizzy over.

She grabs my arms tightly, her sharp nails digging into my skin. "You are to never associate with Sir Vincent Atticus. Do you understand me?" she demands, rage filling her eyes now.

I stay silent, still so confused over her reaction. She continues, "If I ever find out that you have seen him, you will live to regret the very day you were born." Celest stomps away, leaving me more confused and, truthfully, a little curious.

Chapter 5

I jolt awake, sitting upright on the couch, my breath coming in shallow gasps. "Vincent," I whisper, the name lingering on my lips. The man's name is Vincent. And he's a... knight?

Rubbing my eyes hard, I try to comprehend what I have just seen. That was by far the most vivid and life-like dream I've had thus far. But I know now that there isn't anything real about any of this. Nothing could be real about my life in an ancient time that I've never known anything about. And I'm sure as hell not a princess. The very thought makes a giggle form at my lips.

I'm the exact opposite of a princess. Definitely not a leader of any kind. Not even really a follower. I'm more of a lone wolf. A recluse, if you will. And who was that wretched woman? Celest, was it? And she was supposedly my mother?

I can't help but scoff at the idea. Why my mind would make up a woman like that to be my mother, I haven't a clue. My mother is nothing like that Celest woman. She's loving, protective. Maybe too much so. But I've always admired and appreciated everything she's ever done for me. So why dream of her being so awful? None of it makes any sense.

Yet, somehow, what does make sense is my feelings for Vincent. Everything about him was so real. I can still feel his lips on my hand, the tingling growing stronger by the minute. But how could he be real? A knight of all things? Nevertheless, I crave him. I need him.

Feeling defeated, I let out a deep sigh and rest my face in my hands. "I need you, Vincent," I say out loud, my voice echoing softly in the empty room.

I lift my head, realizing how insane I sound, talking to a man that probably doesn't even exist. "Holy Christ, Serenity. You're actually losing your damn mind," I mutter to myself.

My stomach growls in response, and I realize I haven't eaten all day. I look at the clock to see it's almost midnight and figure I better eat and get back to bed.

I look in the fridge to find I have almost nothing to eat. I then realize I really didn't do much shopping in town. I had completely forgotten to get myself any food whatsoever. My mind has been so cluttered lately with everything I've been experiencing. I find a couple of slices of roast beef, left over from last week, and slap it on some stale bread. As I lean against the sink, filling my stomach with this old sandwich, I glance out the window that looks out to the meadow. A soft glow covers the field, lighting up the lone oak tree. Assuming it's just the moon, I don't put much thought into it.

After eating, I head to the bedroom, throwing on pajamas and crawling into bed. I toss and turn for a few hours, unable to sleep. It's so bright outside.

With a huff, I walk over to the window to close the curtain. I glance out, looking for the moon, for I know it must be full. But as I glance around, I notice the moon is nowhere in sight.

Confused, I scan the field to find where the light is coming from. My eyes stop abruptly on the tall oak tree as my breath catches in my chest. I blink a few times, thinking my eyes must be playing tricks on me. But when I open them again, it's still there. A giant ball of white light, about the size of my body, is floating ever so gracefully right next to the beautiful oak, making it glow in a mysterious essence.

"What the hell?" I say aloud. What could this possibly be?

My first thought goes to aliens. Naturally. This is an old farmhouse. Isn't that where all the aliens land? "You're being absurd, Serenity. It's just the light of the moon."

Curiosity getting the best of me, I walk out the back door, stepping onto the dewy grass. I search the sky once more, still having no luck in finding the moon. In fact, it's pitch black out. Only the twinkling of a few stars shining dimly under the thick, black clouds that are rolling in. And the moon is completely covered. This orb, or whatever it is, is something completely different. But what?

I move closer, my head spinning with fear the closer I get to the floating ball of light. I know I should probably turn around and run like hell back to the house. This is like something straight out of a horror film where you get mad at the idiot girl who's dumb enough to go investigate a strange noise in the night. This isn't much different. But I can't seem to stop myself. I feel drawn to it, like it's somehow pulling me in. And the closer I get, the more I notice how beautiful it is. The orb is more like a giant ball of energy, with white lightning coursing through its core.

I draw closer until I'm standing directly in front of it. I cock my head to the side, looking it over and marveling at its beauty. I slowly and cautiously lift my arm, extending it towards the orb. My fingers begin to vibrate in rhythm with the lightning coursing through the light. I'm so close to touching it, I can feel my whole body pulsing with anticipation. I can't help but take one step closer as something inside of me screams to step through it.

My heart begins to drum loudly in my chest, and I smile. I know this feeling. It's the same feeling I have every night in my dreams when I fall asleep. It's love. It's peace. It's home.

Unable to control myself any longer, I muster the courage to finally walk through it. I get one foot in, feeling a rush of energy as it gets engulfed in the orb. But just as I'm about to step completely through, the orb disappears right in front of my eyes, like it never existed at all.

"No!" I cry. "Come back!"

Shocked and grief-stricken, I fall to my knees, scanning every inch of the field. Nothing but total blackness fills the air as silence rings loudly in my ears.

I begin to cry, softly at first, then loud, heart-wrenching sobs begin to seep out. I was so close to where I needed to be. I know it now. I know without a doubt that the orb is my key to finding Vincent. So why wouldn't it let me walk through? Was this just another one of my dreams? I shake my head, knowing better. It couldn't be a dream. I'm fully awake, and I know that. This is different from my dreams.

Feeling defeated, I slump down and lean against the tall oak tree. I sit there for what feels like hours before finally deciding to go back in.

The air has turned chilly, and the dark clouds become thicker as a storm begins to roll in. Feeling uneasy now, I stand and walk quickly to the house. Once inside, I plop down on the bed and stare at the ceiling, then out the window, and back to the ceiling again. I can't fall asleep. I need to wait for the orb to return. If it ever returns. I turn over on my side facing the window, keeping my eyes focused on the big oak in the meadow. The branches move eerily in the night breeze.

I'm determined to stay right here and not move until it comes back. No matter how long it takes.

I wake around ten, the sun peeking through the window and into my drowsy eyes. Frantic that I fell asleep, I jump out of bed and rush to the window, focusing on the tree. Nothing. It's like the light never appeared in the first place. The tall grass sways lazily with the wind, and the leaves dance on its branches. There is nothing out of the ordinary whatsoever. Wouldn't it leave some sort of a trace? Maybe a burn mark in the grass?

I run out of the house and over to the tree, searching around the exact spot I saw the light. There are no traces that anything was ever there. But there was! I saw it. I felt it.

I place both hands on my head and let out a frustrated sigh. How could this be? There has to be a trace of it. Something that big and that powerful feeling didn't just go unnoticed.

Finally giving up, I turn to walk back to the house. But a sparkle on the ground catches my eye. Looking over, I see something small shimmering in the tall grass. I quickly walk over to it and gasp. A beautiful pendant necklace is lying on the grass. The face of it is a big tree, its branches filled with tiny diamonds that shimmer against the sun. I furrow my brow as I look at the necklace and up to the oak tree I'm standing under. Everything about the two is identical. The way the branches sit, right down to the trunk.

Blown away by its beauty, I gently pick it up, the tingling in my hands increasing as I do. I carefully brush the diamonds against my thumb. It feels oddly familiar, like it used to be mine. But I have never seen it before in my life. How did it get here?

Who would have been out here in the field without my knowing it?

I turn the necklace over to inspect it closer, and that's when I see a small engraving.

I love you with all of my heart and soul -V.A

My heart leaps into my chest. V.A. Could that stand for Vincent Atticus? I begin to tremble as I shake the thoughts from my head. How could it? I don't even actually know him. And I have no idea if he even exists, though I feel like he does. This necklace must be nothing more than a coincidence. It must be.

"Serenity!" Sheila yells from the house.

I jump at the sound of my name and look up to see Sheila waving at me. Her face is a mix of concern and curiosity.

Excited to tell someone about what has happened, I half walk, half jog over to my friend. The dew-soaked grass tickles my bare feet, and the early morning sun casts long shadows across the meadow.

"What were you doing way out there?" Sheila asks, looking me over with wide eyes.

I look down and realize I'm only in my bra and underwear, barefoot, and slightly disheveled. Embarrassment flushes my cheeks. "Sheila! You'll never believe what happened last night!" I say, my voice brimming with excitement and urgency.

"What? What happened?" she asks, her brow furrowing in confusion.

"There was a light, right there by that tree!" I say, pointing out to the meadow where the oak tree stands.

"A light?" Sheila raises a brow, skepticism evident in her tone.

"Yes!" I nod fervently, trying to convey the intensity of what I experienced.

"Okay? So, what does that mean? Was someone walking out there?" Sheila asks, looking more puzzled by the second.

"No, no. Nothing like that," I say, waving my hand through the air to dismiss the idea. "It was more like an orb. A giant orb. I think it had something to do with my dreams. It felt..."

"Wait. Stop, Serenity," Sheila interrupts, her expression shifting to one of concern.

I stare at my friend, breathlessly. Sheila stares back, looking nervous, her usual confident demeanor faltering.

"What?" I ask, my voice tinged with anxiety. "Why are you looking at me like that?" I shift my weight from one foot to the next, suddenly feeling uneasy and exposed.

"Ren, what do you mean you saw a light that was connected to your dreams? Do you mean the light was a dream too?" Sheila's voice is cautious, as if she's trying to piece together a puzzle that doesn't make sense.

"No! I had the dream again. But this time I found out his name was Vincent! So then, I wake up and see this light. It felt just like my dreams!" I realize it sounds like I'm talking nonsense, so I stop, taking a deep breath. I look to Sheila again and see a tear trickling down her cheek.

"Sheila?"

"Oh, Ren," Sheila says with a soft sob, her voice breaking.

"I know it sounds crazy, but..."

"*Sounds* crazy?" Sheila raises her voice now, frustration edging into her tone. "Serenity, it *is* crazy! What you saw was just your eyes playing tricks on you. Or maybe a four-wheeler. Did you ever stop to think of that?" She stops to rub her forehead, clearly exasperated. "Ren, it has nothing to do with your dreams. And this Vincent guy? You made him up. You've had so many heartaches; you're trying to create the perfect man in your head."

I wince at her words. Ouch.

"No, Sheila. I really think it's something more. I feel it," I say, my heart pounding in my chest. I need Sheila to believe me.

"Serenity! He. Is. Not. Real," Sheila snaps back, irritation filling her tone.

"Then what about this?" I ask, holding out the necklace to Sheila. She examines it and purses her lips.

"It's beautiful. So what?"

"So what?" I ask, feeling irritation rise in me. "So, look at the initials on the back. V.A."

"So?" Sheila asks, her tone dismissive.

I sigh in frustration. "So, it could stand for Vincent Atticus."

Sheila snaps her head back up to me, anger rising inside of her. She chucks the necklace back to me and throws her hands in the air. "I have to go," she says abruptly.

She storms off before I can get another word in and peels out of the driveway, the sound of her car tires screeching as she speeds away. I stare after her, even though she's long gone. I look around, confused and hurt. What just happened? Why couldn't Sheila just hear me out?

I plop down in the grass, putting my head to my knees and cry. I need just one person in the world to understand me. Or at least attempt to. I need someone to talk to. Not a therapist, obviously. They'd haul me off to a psych ward in a second. I'm well aware that this all sounds absurd. But why couldn't Sheila just listen and try to understand? But if I'm being honest, I can kind of see where Sheila is coming from. It must sound completely insane from her perspective. But it hurts knowing not even my best friend can take me seriously.

After composing myself a little, I wipe the tears away and head back inside to get ready for the day. As I move through my morning routine, I can't help but glance out the window every now and then, hoping to catch a glimpse of the orb again. Just in case.

Chapter 6

I sit at the dinner table, surrounded by my mom and a few of her work colleagues. The room is filled with the soft hum of small talk, occasionally punctuated by bursts of laughter. Every now and then, the conversation shifts to me, with questions that feel more like interrogations than polite inquiries.

"Do you have a boyfriend yet?"

"Don't ask that! Maybe she's into women!"

"When are you getting married?"

"Any kids in your future?"

"How is it being a bartender? Will you be going to college?"

I feel suffocated, the walls closing in as the barrage of questions continues. I want to scream at the top of my lungs and tell everyone to shut the fuck up, but instead, I take a long, deep breath. I don't want to show anger in front of my mom's friends, knowing how it would reflect on her.

I stand from the table, politely excusing myself. I grab a whole bottle of wine and walk out to the patio where I can be alone. I know I have to work later, so I'll drink slowly. It's just a shitty bar anyway, so who really cares?

I take a long sip of wine and look up at the stars twinkling softly against the black sky. The cool night air helps to calm my nerves, and I gently massage my tingling fingers. They've been doing that a lot lately, especially when I'm feeling stressed. And now, a different sensation has started. Since the last dream, my forearm aches so intensely sometimes, it takes my breath away. Though I'll just chalk that up to carpel tunnel. A dream couldn't cause real pain. Maybe that's what the tingling is, too.

I take another sip of wine when my mom comes out, sitting next to me.

"I'm sorry about all the questions. They're just curious," Mom says, her voice soft and apologetic.

"Pretty rude and unnecessary questions, if you ask me," I reply, feeling the frustration still simmering beneath my calm exterior.

Mom purses her lips together as she watches me carefully. "Sheila stopped by today."

I lift my head to look at her. "Oh, God."

"Honey, she was just worried about you. You must understand that."

"I do. But she shouldn't have bothered you. It's nothing," I say in a quiet voice. I know what's coming next. More judgment. More shame. I don't know if I can handle it again, especially from my own mother.

"Sweetheart, it's not nothing. Tell me what the light looked like."

I look up at my mom quizzically. Does she believe me? Or is she just trying to fish for more information so she can determine if I really do belong in a mental hospital?

Feeling skeptical, I begin to explain. "It was big. About as tall as me, maybe. It was white and it looked like it had lightning or something running through it."

Okay, here we go. Lay it on me.

"I believe you," Mom says simply.

I open my mouth to defend myself when I realize what she had just said. Did I just hear her right? "You believe me?" I ask, amazed.

She smiles at me as she caresses my face. "Of course, I do. I've noticed there was something different, special about you since you were a baby. I could see it in your eyes. I could always feel it in your presence." She hesitates for a moment and then sighs. "And I started having dreams, too."

My eyes shoot up to her. "Wh-what kind of dreams?" I ask desperately.

Mom shifts in her seat. "It's weird. It could be nothing. But you were in a castle. And there was this knight named..."

"Vincent," mom and I say in unison.

I let out a gasp as we look at each other in awe.

"Holy fuck," is all I can think to say.

"Language, Serenity!"

"Sorry. But how?"

Mom shakes her head, her eyes scanning the ground like she's frantically trying to think. "I don't know, Ren. I mean I always, for the most part, believed you. But this. This means something." She glances up at me, looking just as shocked as I feel.

"Mom, what does it mean?" I ask, suddenly feeling nervous. I always knew my dreams meant something. But this just proves I've been right all along.

"I don't know, honey. But we're gonna find out together."

"Together?"

"Ren, we had the exact same dream. When was yours?"

"Last night, around eleven."

Her eyes widen. "Mine too. So now that I know I've been right all along in believing you, I think it's time we figure this out."

I touch my forehead, feeling lightheaded. "This is making my head spin."

"I know the feeling."

"Mom, why didn't you ever say before that you believed me?"

"You never asked. And you never really told me that you believed your dreams were real."

That was true. I didn't ever say anything for fear that she would think I was crazy. And that would have broken my heart. I would tell her about some of the dreams I've had, but never how I felt. I've never told her, or anyone. Until this morning when I slipped up with Sheila. Thinking back on this morning makes me cringe. I was just so excited that I found real evidence of something going on. I didn't even stop to think of what the outcome might be.

"I was afraid you'd judge me," I say.

She hugs me tight. "I would never judge you. Not ever."

"What's this?" Mom asks as she touches the necklace around my neck.

"Oh! I found it this morning right where I saw the light. Here, look at the back." I flip it over to show her.

"V.A," she breathes. "Oh my God. Could it be him?"

"What are the odds it could be from someone else? But how did it get there in the middle of the field?"

She shakes her head. "It does seem like too much of a coincidence for it not to be something."

I sigh, nodding in agreement. I'm so relieved that someone actually believes me. Someone I can finally talk to about all of it.

"Oh, and who is that awful woman?" Mom asks, referring to the wretched mother-like figure from the dream.

"I don't know," I chuckle. "But I hope I never meet her."

"Well, if I ever meet her, I'm gonna have to punch her face in for treating you like that," she says as she sits up straight, looking proud.

I let out a laugh. "It was just a dream."

Mom raises her brow. "I think we both know that isn't true."

I nod in agreement. Yes, I do know it's much more than just a dream. I know that now without a shadow of a doubt.

Chapter 7

I feel like a zombie during my shift at the bar, waiting on tables and mixing cocktails without hardly remembering doing so. The cacophony of laughter, clinking glasses, and blaring music melds into a dull, numbing hum around me. I move mechanically, my body on autopilot while my mind is miles away. I don't even notice the men hitting on me or smacking my butt as I walk by them. Or maybe I did notice, but I just don't care anymore. After the evening I have had, with Mom believing me and confessing that she has all along, the not knowing what any of it means, it's all been so much to process. Everything else about my life seems so mundane now, even more so than before. But now I know, without a doubt, that I'm not crazy. I've had so many mixed feelings over it all, oscillating between demanding to myself that this man from my dreams is real and convincing myself I'm crazy all in one go. But now, I have only one thought, one feeling: to find out what all of this means.

And what are the odds that Mom and I would have the exact same dream, on the exact same night, at the exact same time? Astronomical. Maybe vaguely similar dreams could be chalked up to coincidence, but this wasn't vaguely similar. This was exact, right down to every detail, even the names in the dream.

I've never really believed in all this hocus-pocus stuff before. I've always hoped, of course. Most people do hope for the unknown—that somewhere out there is a greater force than just humans behaving like puppets. Drive to work, eat, sleep, repeat, every single day until the day you die. What's the point of all that? So of course, we have an almost burning need to believe in things unknown. But now, I don't have any doubts. As impossible as it seems, I know there is something. But what it is exactly, I have no idea. All I know is, I need to find out soon before I completely lose my mind.

"Sweetheart, wanna come back home with me tonight? I'd like a taste of that sweet ass."

I snap from my thoughts to see a grizzly old man with a tobacco-stained beard and only a few teeth hanging out as he smiles at me. He eyes me up and down, smacking his tongue against the roof of his mouth, and I begin to feel nauseous.

I ignore people hitting on me all the time, even the groping as I walk by the tables. But now, I'm just pissed off.

"Fuck off," I spit as I walk away. I'm done caring what I say to people. I have more important things to worry about now.

"Serenity, I need to see you in the kitchen, please," Harold, my boss, says, his voice cutting through the noise of the bar like a knife.

Great, he must have overheard me, because he's standing in the doorway with his arms crossed, looking displeased. I sigh as I walk over to him, the smell of fryer grease and stale booze growing stronger with each step.

"Yes, sir?" I ask once inside the kitchen, trying to keep my voice steady despite the anger bubbling beneath the surface.

"Serenity, I've talked to you before about how you behave around our customers," he says, arms still crossed and his eyes drilling into mine.

"Yes, sir, I know. But what about their behavior? They have no respect for the women here whatsoever," I retort, my frustration seeping into my words.

"It's your job to tolerate it. Just put a smile on, serve their drinks, and ignore the rest," he says dismissively, as if my concerns are trivial.

I narrow my eyes at him. "So, I'm just supposed to ignore the fact that I get sexually harassed and molested on a nightly basis?" I ask, my voice rising in pitch. "Isn't it the manager's job to ensure his employees work in a safe environment?"

"That's right," he nods, unfazed. "So, if it ever becomes anything more, let me know and I'll handle it. Until then, you have to do your job. Politely."

"Something more?" The next level of this shit would be stalking...or rape!" I say, raising my voice. I'm fuming now, my blood boiling.

Harold sighs. "Serenity, you can either deal with it or not. But this is your last warning. Be nice."

"Or you'll fire me for being harassed," I say. It wasn't a question, for I know it to be true.

"Serenity..."

"No," I say, throwing my hand up to stop him from saying more. "I'm not dealing with it. And I'm sure as hell not gonna put up with a boss who can't protect the women around here. You're just as disgusting as those men out there. And you can fuck right off with them."

Harold stares at me in disbelief, his face turning a shade of red, but I ignore him as I look around the kitchen. Everyone is watching us, their eyes wide with shock and admiration. They smile over at me as if to say, 'someone finally had the balls to stand up to the guy.'

"I'd get the hell out of here if I were you," I say to them. Without another word, I throw my apron down and storm out of the bar, men making kissing and whistling noises all the while.

Once outside on the small cobblestone street, I begin to relax a little. I take in a deep breath as I let the scent of the salty night air fill my lungs and listen to the waves crashing nearby. The night is cool, with a gentle breeze that helps calm my nerves. I can't believe I just quit my job. I had always wanted to tell Harold what I thought of him, and tonight, I finally did it. A small smile forms on my lips as relief floods through me. Maybe now I can concentrate on what the dreams mean, and what to do about them.

Once home, I take my phone out to text Mom:

Thanks for believing in me, Mom. I love you. P.S. I quit my job tonight.

I plop my phone down on the nightstand as I crawl into bed, exhaustion overtaking me. I fall instantly asleep, my dreams waiting to sweep me away once more.

Chapter 8

"Mother, I'm taking Juniper for a ride," I announce as I enter the council room where Mother Celest is sitting with my uncle, Sir Edmond, discussing preparations for increased military training. The room is filled with the scent of old parchment and the low murmur of serious conversation.

"Fine, dear. Just take a guard with you," she says, waving me away with a flick of her wrist as she resumes sifting through papers, clearly signaling that she's done talking to me.

I roll my eyes at her and make my way through the long, winding hallways and down the spiraling stone stairs. The cool, ancient stones of the castle walls feel grounding beneath my fingers as I trace them absentmindedly. Two guards open the massive double doors for me to exit, and I thank them kindly before striding out to the palace steps.

It's a beautiful day for a ride. The sun is shining brightly, and a gentle breeze carries the scent of blooming flowers and freshly cut grass. Plus, I really need to clear my head. Since meeting Sir Vincent, I haven't been able to think of anything else. The intense passion and connection I feel towards him takes my breath away. I want more than anything to talk to him and to be around him. But for whatever reason, Mother forbade it.

I can still see the look in Mother's eyes as she first laid eyes on Vincent. The sheer terror that crossed her expression has baffled me. I have never seen her afraid of anything, much less a knight. She had never been afraid of even the most ruthless leaders who have come after her in the past. She simply struck them down without a second thought. So, what was it about this knight? What could possibly be so terrifying? Whatever the reason, he scared the hell out of her, and I'm intrigued by it. Not only because Mother acts so strangely around him, but because it's like something is pulling me towards Vincent. And I can't stop it, even if I wanted to. Which I don't. I have this intense desire to be around him, and I have no idea why.

Sure, he's handsome. Very handsome, in fact. His chiseled jawline, piercing green eyes, and that rugged stubble makes my heart flutter. But that's no reason to be irresistibly drawn to someone. I usually have so much self-control. But when it comes to Sir Vincent, I feel like I have none. I need more than anything to talk to him. But how?

Once at the stables, I fetch my beloved horse. Juniper has been my best friend over the years. Her sleek brown coat glistens in the sunlight, and her gentle eyes meet mine as I approach. I've always felt so alone. My father died when I was only two, and since then, it's been just Mother and me. But

Mother never cared one way or another that Father was gone, so I couldn't even share grief of being fatherless with her.

I do have Uncle, though, whom I can talk to about anything. He has always kept my secrets and given advice, especially on how to deal with Mother. And just recently, Lady Arain had come into my life to serve me. Though, I've never thought of her as a servant. I've only ever thought of her as a friend. We've grown close over the past few months, and of course, Mother cannot seem to fathom why I would make friends with a serving girl. She has always said that servants were meant to serve; they aren't capable of becoming friends.

The more I think of how wicked my mother is, the more I want to run away from here and never return. But she would never allow it. She'd hunt me down and drag me back.

"Hi, June bug," I say as I pet Juniper's soft brown face. "How would you like to go for a ride?"

Juniper lets out a small neigh in agreement, and I can't help but smile at her. I begin saddling her up, the familiar routine calming my restless mind.

"Your Highness." My heart begins to flutter, for I would recognize that voice anywhere.

"Sir Vincent," I say with a smile as I turn around to greet him.

His eyes twinkle as he gives a flashing smile, making me weak in the knees. "Going for a ride?" he asks, nodding his head toward Juniper.

"I am..." I say in anticipation.

He smiles sheepishly as he draws closer to me. "Would you care for some company?" he asks.

My heart begins to race faster, and my skin burns hot. Mother said to stay away from him. But was it really necessary? She did say to bring a guard with me. So, I am doing what she asked. Kind of.

And, if he were dangerous, Uncle would have never named him a knight of Duix.

I know Mother would probably have me killed or locked away for being seen with him, but I really don't care. I can't help myself. I feel a strong pull towards this mysterious man. My entire body tingles when he's near, almost like something is alive within me.

"I would love some," I say as I look him over. My eyes finally land on his, and I notice him watching me, a devilish smile spreading across his face. I blush, looking down at the ground.

Sir Vincent clears his throat. "Shall we be on our way, then?"

The sun is shining brightly, and a gentle breeze sweeps across my face. The forest floor is plush and vibrant this time of year. Flowers of all colors poke out of the ground, and vines wrap themselves snugly around trees. Birds sing nearby, and little squirrels scurry around in search of food. It's like something from a fairytale.

We come to a clearing in the woods, a small pond positioned in the middle. The water ripples softly, making it sparkle like hundreds of tiny diamonds.

"Why don't we stop here?" I suggest as I stroke Juniper's head. "Juniper needs a drink anyway."

"Of course, your Highness," Sir Vincent says as he jumps off his own horse, striding over to me in one smooth motion.

I put my hand in his and gently squeeze. He puts his arm around my waist, setting me on the ground just as smoothly. I can't help but stare into his eyes. They're easily becoming my greatest addiction.

I'm close enough to take in his sweet and masculine scent. I breathe him in as I briefly close my eyes, not wanting this exact moment to end. Being this close to him makes me feel things I've never felt before. I didn't think it was possible for a feeling like this to exist, but here I am, falling head over heels for a man I have only just met.

I feel foolish for feeling so strongly for him. He probably doesn't feel the same way about me. How could he? We don't know a thing about one another. So, how is it possible for me to feel this way? I find him completely irresistible, alluring even. I have been courted by men before, some Mother knew about, some she didn't. But never before have I felt anything this strong.

Realizing I still have my arm around his neck, and his arm around my waist, I back away, embarrassed.

"Shall we sit by the water, Your Highness?" Sir Vincent asks as he pulls a blanket out of his pack.

I glance over at him. "You really don't have to keep calling me that, you know. You may call me

Serenity," I say as I sit on the blanket that's sprawled over the grass.

"I wouldn't want to be disrespectful," he says as he sits next to me.

He focuses his eyes on my lips, and I instinctively begin to nibble them softly. His gaze slowly lifts to mine, causing a fire to ignite deep within my soul.

"That may be true," I say. "But I don't like when my friends call me that."

"Your friend?" he asks, surprised.

"Well, I hope for you to be. You intrigue me, Sir Vincent Atticus of House Brelin," I say, not taking my eyes off him.

He smiles at me softly. "You remember where I'm from?"

"Of course," I say, smiling back. I want more than anything to reach out and touch his stubble-covered face. To feel his skin against mine. It's taking all the power I have within me not to, as my heart aches for his touch.

"You intrigue me, too, Serenity," he says as he searches my eyes with his.

"I do?"

"Yes. There's just something. I... well, I can't explain it," he stammers.

I feel my face flush as I look into his bold eyes. "I know exactly what you mean," I say in a half-whisper.

We sit in silence together for the rest of the time, staring out at the shimmering pond. We watch as the horses drink from the cool water, looking as if they don't have a care in the world.

Everything feels right in this moment as I sit side by side with him. I feel like my true self is finally shining through for the very first time. I don't have to pretend with him. I don't have to be someone I'm not. I'm just... me.

As I look up at the sun beginning to sink low to the west, I can't help but feel disappointment. I never want my time to end with Vincent, but I know Mother will be wondering where I am if I don't get back. The last thing I need is for her to find us together. Who knows what would happen? My heart sinks at the very thought of her evil wrath against Sir Vincent. Whatever it is she has against him, it's making me feel wildly protective of him.

I glance over at him, peace crossing his face as a small smile plays at his lips. The serene expression makes my heart flutter even more. "Shall we be going, Sir Vincent? I have to be getting back to the castle soon," I say, my voice tinged with reluctance.

A glimpse of disappointment crosses his once peaceful face, and I try to ignore it so the stinging in my heart might subside. He catches himself quickly and offers me a smile. "Of course, your hi—Serenity," he corrects himself, the warmth in his eyes returning.

I let out a small laugh as I look into his eyes, feeling a connection that goes beyond mere words. He reaches up to brush the hair out of my face, and when his skin meets mine, I feel soft pulses of electricity coursing through me. It wasn't from the excitement; this was something more. Much more. Whatever it is, it feels like my whole body is soaring. I take in a sharp breath as I look up at him. He's staring at me with such passion in his eyes that I feel I might burst.

And in that moment, as bizarre as it might sound, I am sure I have just fallen madly in love with him.

"What… my gods, what was that?" he asks breathlessly, his eyes searching mine for answers.

"I have no idea," I say in a whisper, trying to still my fluttering heart. The intensity of the moment leaves me breathless, and I can see he's feeling it too.

Curious to see if it would happen again, I softly touch his face next, like I have been craving to do all day. The sensation is immediate. Electricity, fire, passion. It all comes crashing through my body at once. His skin is warm and inviting, and I can't help but let my fingers linger on his cheek. By the look on Vincent's face, it's happening to him again too. He draws closer to me, his face only inches from mine. I can feel his breath playing against my lips, warm and enticing, sending shivers down my spine. I reach up, placing my hand around the back of his neck as I lean my forehead against his. His hair is soft between my fingers, and I can feel the tension and desire radiating from him.

I want more than anything to kiss him right now. But I know it wouldn't be right. We have just met, and this was really the first time we've ever truly talked to one another. Part of me is afraid. Afraid that if his lips were to touch mine, I might explode into tiny bits. Not to mention what would happen if Mother ever found out. I couldn't let this happen. Not now anyway. I care too deeply for him. The very thought of all the things that could go wrong with this is enough to stop me.

But I still wanted, needed *to be close to him. Just for a moment anyway. His presence soothes me in a way I've never felt before.*

"As much as I want to stay like this forever, I really have to be getting back to the castle," I say, trying to ignore the intense feeling bubbling up inside me. The words are heavy on my tongue, filled with reluctance and longing.

"Certainly," he says in a husky tone. His voice sends another wave of warmth through me. He searches my eyes once more before saying, "maybe we can go for another ride tomorrow?"

I smile wide, unable to hide my excitement. I know it isn't safe for anyone involved. "I would love to," I say. I can't seem to stop myself. The words come out before I have the chance to change my mind. I know, without a doubt, I have to see him again.

The sun is now sinking lower, casting long shadows across the clearing. The golden light dances on the surface of the pond, creating a mesmerizing display of sparkles. The birds have quieted, and the air is filled with the sounds of the forest preparing for nightfall. The serenity of the moment contrasts sharply with the storm of emotions swirling inside me.

What a fitting name for me to have. Serenity.

As we mount our horses and begin the ride back to the castle, I can't help but steal glances at Sir Vincent. His strong, confident posture, the way he handles his horse with such ease, and the way he occasionally looks over at me with that soft, almost tender expression—it all makes my heart race even more.

The ride back feels shorter, too short, and before I know it, the castle looms ahead. The imposing structure, with its tall spires and thick walls, seems almost foreboding now. A stark reminder of the world I must return to, away from the enchanting moments with Vincent.

We dismount, and I hand Juniper off to a stable hand. Vincent stands close, his presence comforting yet electrifying. "Thank you for the ride, Serenity. It was... incredible," he says, his voice low and sincere.

"It was," I agree, feeling a pang of sadness that the ride is over. "Until tomorrow, Sir Vincent."

"Until tomorrow," he echoes, and with one last lingering look, we part ways.

As I walk back into the castle, the reality of my situation begins to settle in. But now, there's a spark of something new. Hope. Curiosity. A burning desire to understand the connection I feel with Sir Vincent. Whatever it takes, I know I must explore this further, even if it means defying my mother.

I take a deep breath and step into the dimly lit hallway of the castle, the warmth of the encounter still coursing through me, fueling my resolve.

Chapter 9

I gasp as I awaken, my heart still hammering in my chest. I can still feel the vibration of Vincent's touch, the warmth of his flesh lingering on my fingertips as if he were still there. I let out a shaky breath as I sit up in bed, the moonlight casting eerie shadows across my room. The dreams are becoming more and more lifelike. If they become any more vivid, I might have a hard time distinguishing between a dream and reality. But they aren't just dreams. Vincent is real. And as crazy as it sounds, our love for each other is real.

I crawl out of bed, the cool floorboards creaking under my feet, and grab a glass of water. The house is silent, the only sound the distant ticking of the grandfather clock in the hallway. I notice it isn't yet light out and glance at the clock as I make my way to the bathroom sink. Three in the morning. I still have a few hours of sleep left, but I'm not sure I'll be able to. Not now. Not after the dream I just had. My mind keeps spinning around the thought of Vincent. I miss him.

"God, Serenity. You sound like a raging lunatic," I say to myself in the mirror, my reflection looking back at me with tired, disheveled eyes. How is it possible to miss someone you don't even know?

As I go to take a sip of water, I see a reflection of something in the bathroom mirror. Startled, I quickly turn to see what appears to be an empty room. My heart races as I cautiously walk forward, the shadows playing tricks on my mind.

"Hello?" I call out, my voice barely above a whisper. Silence.

I quickly glance around the room once more, but I don't see anything out of place. Chalking it up to nothing more than my imagination, I crawl back into bed and grip the diamond necklace I found in the field. It soothes me knowing that it could have come from Vincent.

Just as I start to drift to sleep once more, I hear a noise coming from my room. My eyes pop open as I sit up in bed, adrenaline coursing through my veins. The room feels colder, and I get the strange sense that I'm being watched. I scan the dark room again, my eyes adjusting to the dim light. But this time, as I get to the far corner by the window, I see a shadow of a... person? I quickly flick the lights on, and there, in the corner, is Mom smiling as she stares at me. My stomach drops as dread fills my stomach.

"Momma?" I ask cautiously, my voice trembling.

"Hello, my dear, sweet Serenity. It's been a long time," she says as she walks closer to me. Her voice sounds different somehow, more hateful and cold.

I quickly fumble out of bed, my pulse quickening. "What do you mean, Momma? I just saw you tonight."

"Oh, no, sweetheart. That wasn't me," she says in a chilling tone that makes the hair on the back of my neck stand up.

"I... I don't know what's going on here," I say in a shaky tone, my mind racing.

"Look at you. Still so weak. Still so pitiful," she says disapprovingly, her eyes narrowing.

My stomach turns to knots as I stare at her. "I get the feeling I'm not talking to my mom," I say cautiously, taking a step back.

"Oh, but you are, dear! It's Mommy Celest. Don't I get a hug after all these years?" she says, her voice dripping with sarcasm.

I feel the blood drain from my face. Did she just say... Celest? The evil woman from my dreams? How could that possibly be?

I straighten, trying not to seem so nervous. "Celest, what are you doing here?"

She steps closer to me, her glare intense. "I'm here to tell you to stay the hell away from that light."

I try to hide the shock on my face. "How do you know about...?"

Celest cuts me off by putting up a hand. "I don't know how those memories are returning to you, and I don't know how you're conjuring the light. I did everything in my power to ensure that would never happen. But I'm here to tell you, if you ever cross through, I will make your life a living hell. I will hunt you down, Serenity. I will slaughter every single person you hold dear. Starting with your precious uncle. And oh, the things I'll do to Vincent! Unimaginable... horrible things."

I only stare at her, not fully comprehending everything Celest just said. Memories? They aren't dreams but... memories? I have so many questions, but I can't open my mouth to speak. I just stand there, frozen with fear.

A wicked smile crosses Celest's face. "I see you don't exactly remember who you are. That's good. The old you would have had a sly remark by now."

I open my mouth to try to speak again, but nothing comes out. As I stare at my innocent mother, I see the hatred of Celest shining through.

Celest sighs. "I told you to stay away from him, Serenity. But you never listen to Mommy."

Before I can try to get a word in, Mom falls to the floor.

"Mom!" I yell as I fall to my knees next to her. Her eyes open as she looks up at me. I let out a sigh of relief. This looks more like my mom. Not so evil. Not so full of hate.

"What the hell just happened?" Mom asks as she frantically looks around the room.

"You wouldn't believe me if I told you," I say, because I hardly believe it myself. I'm still mostly convinced it was just another dream.

"It was Celest, wasn't it?"

"How did you...?" I couldn't finish my sentence. She knows Celest's name now? My head begins to spin. This is far too much excitement for one day.

"I felt her, Ren. She's so full of hate. She hates everyone and everything. She despises you and Vincent the most. She fears you."

My eyes widen as I let out a nervous giggle. "Fears me?"

Mom nods her head. "That's what it felt like."

I slump down on the floor next to her. "Mom, I don't understand any of this! Is Celest really my mother? Did you adopt me? How did she erase my memories?" I'm so frantic now, I begin to cry. Between sobs I say, "And how in the actual fuck did she jump ship to your body?"

She scoops me in her arms and kisses my forehead. "Sweety, you weren't adopted. I spent three grueling days in the hospital to have you. And you remember your childhood with me. As for everything else, I have no idea. But we will get to the bottom of this."

I nod my head, letting her comfort me. I'm not sure how we'll ever get to the bottom of it, but my mom has always had a way of making me feel like everything is going to be okay.

She lets go of me now as she looks at me. "Now, I think we should have a little girl time. Just me and you."

"It's four in the morning," I say, raising a brow at her.

"I know that," she says, rolling her eyes. "We're going to sit out back and wait for the light to return."

I smile wide. "You're the greatest mom ever. Did you know that?"

"Hm. Much better than that bitch, Celest."

I raise a brow at her, shocked that she swore. She's always so against me swearing and scolds me anytime I slip up.

"What? I learn from the best," Mom says as she walks toward the back door. "Plus, who does she think she is taking over my body like that?" she asks with a shiver.

We sit in the tall grass, leaning our backs against the oak tree. The night is blacker than normal, almost as though Celest left part of her evil behind.

"Do you think the dreams are really memories?" I ask Mom.

She sits silent for a moment, staring out into the darkness. "I don't know, Ren. I don't see how they could be." She shakes her head as if to clear her thoughts. "Then again, I don't see how we could have the same dreams and be possessed by a crazy lady, but here we are."

I nod in agreement. Nothing about this makes sense. There's no way they could be memories. I remember every detail of my childhood. I remember Momma cooking meals every evening and sharing funny stories about our day. I remember being home from school while I was sick. Momma stayed by my side the whole time, never leaving me. I never knew my father. Mom wasn't so sure herself who he was. It's not that she was going around being with a bunch of different men. She said she found out she was pregnant a couple months after a party she was at, having no recollection of the events leading up to her pregnancy. I've always felt tinged with guilt, knowing I am more than likely a product of rape. Though mom never made me feel that she resented me. The opposite in fact. She has always been so loving and nurturing.

All of that, I know to be real. But my dreams, they feel real too. How is it possible? They are so much more than just made-up images in my head. I know that to be true too. But how?

"I had another dream tonight," Mom says, snapping me from my thoughts.

"Me too. What was yours?"

"You went for a ride on Juniper. Vincent accompanied you," she says, smiling like she's recalling a fond memory.

I swallow hard. None of this seems possible. But here we are, face to face with the impossible.

"The pond was so beautiful," I say, smiling now.

"It was," Mom agrees.

I look over at her, and she seems lost deep in her thoughts. When she catches me staring, she says, "You and Vincent have something unlike anything I've ever seen before. And what was that feeling? It was like electricity."

I sigh fondly. "I don't know. But I want it back," I say, my voice filled with longing. The memory of the electric touch and the intense connection with Vincent lingers, making my heart ache for more.

Mom nods in agreement, her expression thoughtful. "Do you think it's some kind of magic?" she asks, her tone curious and a bit skeptical.

I raise a brow at her, not saying anything as a small smile plays at my lips. The idea of magic has always seemed ridiculous to me, something out of fairy tales and stories, not real life.

"Well!" Mom continues, leaning in closer as if sharing a secret. "How else would you explain all of this? The feelings between the two of you, Celest coming here, the dreams?"

"I can't explain any of it," I admit, frustration creeping into my voice. "But how could it be magic? Is there even really such a thing? And why just now? Why didn't it happen before?" My hands begin to tingle fiercely. Frustrated, I rub them together, trying to ease the sensation that feels like tiny sparks under my skin.

"Maybe it's just happening now because it's the right time," she suggests, her eyes searching mine for understanding.

"Time for what?" I ask, feeling a knot of anxiety tightening in my stomach.

"I have no idea," she admits with a sigh, her shoulders slumping slightly.

We sit in silence for a while, staring out at the black field. The night is alive with the soft glow of fireflies lighting up the tall grass, their tiny lights flickering like stars falling to earth. I smile at the sight of them, finding a small bit of peace in their presence.

I go over every detail of the last dream I had in my head. I need to see Vincent again. I am so ridiculously in love with the man, and I have no idea where he even is. But I'm sure the light has something to do with it. Why else would Celest have been so upset about it? I just hope that it returns so I can find out.

"Do you really think I'm a princess?" I ask with a smirk, the thought alone seeming absurd. The idea of me, Serenity, a less-than-average girl from a small town in Maine who no one really notices, being a princess is laughable.

"God, I hope so!" Mom exclaims, her laughter infectious. We both laugh, the sound echoing in the still night air, momentarily easing the tension the night has brought us.

As we sit by the oak tree for a while longer, I begin to lose all hope of ever seeing the light again. I let out a sigh, feeling disappointment and a little anger bubbling up inside me.

"Mom, the light isn't coming. Plus, the sun will be up soon," I say, impatiently plucking the grass out of the ground and tossing it aside.

"I wouldn't be so sure about that, Ren," she replies, her tone mysterious.

I look up at her, and she nods her head towards the field.

I snap my head up to the field, and there, right in front of me, is a small ball of light next to the big tree. I slowly stand, as Mom follows suit. The light flickers once, and I think it has disappeared completely. I take a big, frantic step forward, my heart pounding in my chest.

"Don't be afraid of it, Ren. Believe in it. Feel it. And it will return to you," Mom says, her voice steady and reassuring.

"How do you know that?" I ask her, my voice barely a whisper.

"I don't know. I just do," she replies, her eyes fixed on the glowing orb.

I close my eyes and think of the light, and of Vincent. I think of the love I feel for him, and the way his skin feels against mine. I let the feelings wash over me, and I truly believe it's real.

When I open my eyes, the light has returned to me. Brighter and stronger this time. It begins to grow to the size it was when I first saw it. The little lightning-like streaks course through it, making my entire soul burn with excitement.

"It's time for you to go, Ren," Mom says, her voice tinged with awe as she stares at the light.

I look over to her, and she's watching it carefully. It's like she's being drawn to it too, like she somehow has knowledge of it.

"Come with me," I plead as I grab both of her hands in mine, my voice trembling with emotion.

Mom shakes her head gently. "You need to do this alone. I can feel it," she says, her eyes meeting mine with a mixture of sadness and resolve.

I look at her quizzically, so she continues, "I have no idea how I know. I just do. Now you must go."

A tear slips from my eye, rolling down my cheek. "I'll come back for you, Momma," I promise, my voice breaking.

"I know. I can feel that too," she says with a reassuring smile, squeezing my hands tightly.

I hug her tight, feeling the warmth and comfort of her embrace. "Thank you. Thank you for believing in me and always being by my side."

"I will always believe in you, my sweet daughter. I love you so much," she whispers, her voice filled with love and conviction.

"I love you," I say, my voice choked with emotion. "I'll see you soon."

I turn towards the light, facing it head-on. I step a little closer, feeling oddly confident in myself. It's as though the light is mine, and I'm going home. The closer I get, the more intense the vibration courses through my body. One more step, and I'll be inside. Just one more step, and I'll hopefully find the answers I've been so desperately searching for.

I look back to my mom, and she gives me a reassuring nod, her eyes filled with pride and hope. I take a deep breath and step through, the light enveloping me in its warmth. Everything goes black around me, and I feel myself being pulled into the unknown.

Chapter 10

"Uncle, may I come in?" I ask as I tap lightly on the door to his chambers, my voice trembling slightly with uncertainty.

"Come in!" he calls, his voice warm and welcoming.

I push the door open and cautiously step inside, the scent of old parchment and ink filling my senses. Candles lit and scattered around, casting a warm, golden glow over the room. Uncle Edmond sits at his large wooden desk, cluttered with papers and books. The room is lined with shelves filled with ancient tomes and military artifacts, a testament to his long and distinguished career.

"Sit down, my dear," he says, motioning towards the chair in front of his desk.

I notice he looks busy. Papers are sprawled out across his desk, and a pen is in his hand, pausing mid-sentence. Uncle Edmond is a handsome middle-aged man with short, black hair and a black beard, with gray scattered throughout. He's tall and buff from all his years in the military, and his eyes are fierce and bright green. But under all of that, is a gentle soul. He would do anything for anyone, especially when it came to me. He has always taken care of me when Celest wouldn't. He has always made sure I had everything I've ever needed. When I was a child, he would have dinner with me and tuck me into bed, telling me soothing bedtime stories to fall asleep to. Since my father died when I was so young, Uncle has taken on the role nicely.

"Maybe I should come back later," I suggest, seeing the mountain of work before him and not wanting to be a burden.

Uncle scoffs with a wave of his hand. "Nonsense. I always have time for you," he says, setting down his pen and giving me his full attention.

I give a soft smile as I look down at my trembling hands. I twist them together, hoping to hide my jumbled nerves from him. The cool, smooth texture of the chair's armrests is a small comfort.

Uncle furrows his brow, concern etching lines into his forehead. "Serenity, dear. What's troubling you?" he asks gently.

"It's... it's kind of hard to talk about," I mumble, my voice barely above a whisper.

Fear flashes across his face. "Did something happen? Were you hurt?" he asks, his tone urgent and protective.

"No, no. Nothing like that, Uncle," I assure him quickly, wanting to ease his worry.

He relaxes a little as he sits back in his chair, the tension in his shoulders easing. "You know you can talk to me about anything," he presses, his voice steady and reassuring.

"Well, it's about Vincent. Sir Vincent, that is," I begin, my heart racing as I finally broach the subject.

"Okay... what about him?" he asks, leaning forward in his chair, his eyes poking out above his glasses, curiosity mingling with concern.

I decide I can't hold it in any longer and let it all spill out. "Mother demands that I stay away from him. She threatened bodily harm, if you can believe it," I say, my voice shaking with frustration and fear. Uncle huffs, rolling his eyes. He knows how impossible Celest can be, just as I do.

"I intended on obeying her, but I couldn't. From the moment I met him that first day, there was something that lured me in. I'm in love with him, Uncle," I confess, my face flushing as I say the last part. I've never said it out loud before. I've never even told Vincent.

Uncle's eyes soften as he speaks. "You and Sir Vincent have been spending some time together, then?" he asks, his tone gentle.

I look down at my hands, feeling the weight of my confession. "Yes, some," I admit. After our first ride together, we have spent almost every day together. Not always for long. Just a quick 'hello' or a walk through the courtyard when I knew no one was around to see.

But despite the small amount of time we have been together, my feelings grow stronger for him each day.

I let out a sigh. "What do I do, Uncle? I know it's wrong. I'm a princess. He's a knight. And Mother is going to kill me if she finds out."

"You let me worry about Celest," he says with a determined look.

I only smile, still feeling defeated. There is nothing Uncle can say or do to change Celest's mind.

He continues, "Now, as far as you being a princess and he a knight, that doesn't matter. Not to me, anyway. Love is often found in the most unusual places, Ren. And you can't help who it's with."

"Mother would have your head if she heard you say that," I tease, though I'm not entirely sure it wasn't true. Celest would have anyone's head if it suited her.

"Yes, she probably would," Uncle agrees with a chuckle. "Just be careful about it for now. Don't let her catch you with him. I'll get to the bottom of what's troubling your mother. Though I can't begin to imagine what she would have against Sir Vincent."

"Did I hear something about Sir Vincent?"

I jump as dread fills my heart and my blood runs cold in my veins. I look up to see Mother standing in the doorway, arms crossed, her eyes narrowing at us.

Uncle and I glance at each other before he looks back to Mother.

"We were just discussing the upcoming training event. Sir Vincent is part of that, as you well know,"

Uncle says, sounding as convincing as he can. I just pray for his sake that Mother believes him.

"Serenity, leave us," Mother says, her voice cold and commanding.

I begin to shake as I slowly stand from my chair. And as I turn to leave, Mother grabs me hard by my arms, her grip like iron, glaring at me with fury in her eyes.

"If I find out you so much as made eye contact with that man, I will throw you in the cells and have your head on a pike. Do you hear me?" Celest says, shaking me viciously, her nails digging into my skin.

My nervousness quickly turns to anger as I glare at her, hate filling my heart. "By all means. We wouldn't want to upset her majesty," I say in a sarcastic tone as I curtsey, my voice dripping with disdain.

Celest smacks me hard, right above my eyes. My vision blurs with the blood pouring down my face, and I grab my eye, staring at her in shock. And now I know from this moment on, she is no longer my mother. She is no longer my queen.

She is my enemy.

"I am not just your mother. I am your queen first, and you will show me respect, you pitiful little cockroach," Celest yells, her voice echoing through the chamber.

"Celest, damn it! Stop this right now!" Uncle yells as he slams his fists down on the desk and abruptly stands from his chair, his voice filled with rage.

I don't hear anything else that's being said. I'm seeing red, quite literally, and shaking with the adrenaline coursing through my veins. I run from Uncle's room, down the winding hallways, and out the front door. I want to find Vincent, but I know Celest will be looking for me as soon as she's done with Uncle. The blood drains from my face at the thought of what might happen to him. I need to go check on him later, because it would not surprise me if Celest threw him in the cells to be executed. She has killed for much less.

Once in the stables, I sit in the hay where Juniper lies sleeping. I stroke his soft fur while he takes deep, rhythmic breaths. The scent of hay and horses fills the air, a comforting, familiar aroma. Being in the stables always calms me, and I find myself out here more frequently. Anytime Celest decides to execute an innocent man, or when she goes off on tangents telling me how pitiful I am, I would be here. I can't stand her. And being hit in the face was the last straw.

"Serenity?" Vincent asks in a concerned tone, his voice like a soothing balm to my raw emotions.

I look up to see him standing in the doorway. He's so tall and so handsome. And his armor makes him look fierce and strong, like a warrior from a legend.

"Hi," I say, as a tear runs down my cheek, the pain and fear of the evening catching up to me.

"Serenity, what happened?" he asks as he quickly reaches me, his eyes filled with concern.

As he examines my bruised and bloody eye, anger flashes across his face, his jaw clenching tightly.

"Who did this to you, Ren?" he asks, his voice low and dangerous, his hand resting softly on my cheek, his touch gentle despite his fury.

"Celest," I say as I touch my hand to his, the connection between us giving me strength.

"Why would she do something like this to her own daughter?" he asks, disbelief and anger mingling in his voice.

"Because I talked back to her. She's so concerned about whether I've been seeing you. She told me to stay away from you or she'd hurt us both." Another tear slips down my cheek, and he wipes it away with his thumb, his touch tender and soothing.

"Why?" he asks, confusion and anger mingling in his voice.

"I don't know," I say as I stand, brushing the hay from my dress. "She told me to stay away from you the first day you came here. It doesn't make any sense."

"No, it doesn't," he replies thoughtfully. "I don't think my family ever knew yours before coming here. So why would she have anything against me?"

"I don't know. But I'm going to find out," I say, feeling the anger welling up inside me again.

"Ren, you don't have to go through this trouble for me," he says, pain flashing across his face, his eyes searching mine for understanding.

"Yes, I do!" I say, my voice firm and unwavering.

"Why, Ren?" he asks as he steps closer to me, his eyes burning with passion, making me weak in the knees. The intensity of his gaze sends shivers down my spine.

I let out a huff, my heart pounding in my chest. "Isn't it obvious? No matter how hard I might try, I can't stay away from you. I am so irresistibly, and madly in love with you, Vincent. I can't just let you go. I won't!" I say, breathlessly, my words tumbling out in a rush of emotion.

Vincent steps closer until the warmth of his skin radiates into mine, his presence overwhelming. A small smile plays at the corner of his lips as he brushes my face with his fingers, his touch sending sparks through my skin. "You mean the entire world to me, Serenity. I've never loved anything or anyone as much as I love you," he whispers, his voice thick with passion.

My heart begins to pound harder as he leans in close to me, our lips only inches apart. I place my hand on his face, caressing the coarse stubble that covers his chin, feeling the rough texture under my fingertips. I can't take it anymore. I have to kiss him. I slowly reach up, pressing my lips to his, creating an explosion deep within my soul. I could swear the ground is shaking beneath our feet, but I assume it's nothing more than the adrenaline coursing through my veins.

Vincent backs away for a moment to look into my eyes, his gaze intense and filled with longing. He wraps his arms tighter around me and whispers, "Oh, Serenity."

He kisses me deeper now, with such urgency and passion that my whole body begins to tremble. My skin begins to burn hot, the sensation so intense that it feels like my very soul is on fire. It's the most incredible feeling I've ever experienced. He must be feeling it too because we look down at the same time. What I see takes my breath away. We're both glowing a pale yellow, as though our blood is being lit up by some kind of light and radiating through our skin. I feel a faint tinge of pain on my forearm. As I look down, a small tree inked in black forms. Vincent looks down astonished at what he's seeing as he lifts his arm up to mine. I gasp as I realize what is happening. He too has a small tree etched into his skin in the exact same spot as mine. I don't know how it's even possible. But for some reason, I don't question it. It feels natural, like it's now a part of who we are.

And it's in that moment, I know, there is something magical between us. The air around us seems to shimmer with energy, and the world fades away until there is nothing but Vincent and me, connected in a way that defies explanation. The glow intensifies, bathing us in its ethereal light, and I feel a profound sense of belonging, as if I've finally found the missing piece of myself.

Vincent pulls back slightly, his eyes wide with wonder. "Do you feel that?" he asks, his voice a hushed whisper.

"Yes," I breathe, my heart racing. "It's like we're connected on a whole different level."

He nods, his expression one of awe. "I've never felt anything like this before. It's like our souls are intertwined."

I smile, feeling a surge of joy and relief. "It's real, Vincent. This connection between us... it's real."

He cups my face in his hands, his touch tender and reverent. "I love you, Serenity. With everything that I am."

Tears well up in my eyes as I reach up to touch his face, mirroring his gesture. "And I love you, Vincent. More than words can say."

We stand there, wrapped in each other's arms, the glow slowly fading but the connection between us remaining strong. In that moment, I know that no matter what challenges lie ahead, we will face them together. Because our love is not just a fleeting emotion—it's a force of nature, a magic all its own.

Chapter 11

My eyes pop open. My vision is blurred, and my body feels buzzed. I blink a few times, slowly bringing into focus the blue sky above me, and a plush, green forest surrounding me. The air is cool and crisp, carrying the scent of pine and wildflowers. I quickly sit up, immediately regretting it as a wave of dizziness hits me. I touch my hand to my forehead until the spinning subsides.

"What the hell just happened?" I ask myself, my voice echoing softly through the trees.

I open my eyes again to take in my surroundings. It's so beautiful. The trees are tall, with red bark and deep green, bushy leaves. The ground is covered in moss that squishes softly beneath my feet, feeling like a soft, natural carpet. Wildflowers dot the forest floor, scattered in big, vibrant patches of purples, yellows, and blues. It looks and feels so much like my dreams.

My dreams!

"Oh, my God!" I say frantically as I quickly glance around.

It's all coming back to me now. Sitting by the oak tree with my mom, and the light. I stepped through it, and now I'm in the middle of the woods. Could it be that this is the place I have seen so many times before? Or did I fall asleep, and this is just another dream?

No, this definitely isn't a dream. I know it isn't. This feels different. It feels real. I can smell the wildflowers and the fresh air. Everything is so clear and vivid. This is real. My dreams had never been like this.

I take in a deep breath and close my eyes. I've never felt so alive. So peaceful. So powerful. The sounds of birds chirping and leaves rustling in the gentle breeze fill the air.

"Vincent!" I say in a panic. "I need to find Vincent."

I quickly stand and begin jogging through the forest, having no idea where I even am or if I'm close to home. All I really know is that I'm where I'm supposed to be. Something inside of me is screaming it. And then it tells me to go straight. I obey the feeling inside of me, for I know it'll lead me straight to Vincent.

The sun begins to set under the trees, casting long shadows that dance across the forest floor. The sky transforms into a canvas of oranges and pinks. I realize I must find shelter quickly. But how is it dark already? It was almost daylight just moments ago with my mom. Could it be that I was passed out for a whole day?

I let out a frustrated huff. The sky is darker now, and the forest seems darker yet. Oddly enough though, I'm not afraid. The Serenity I know is afraid of the dark, especially in an unfamiliar place I've never been before. Or maybe I have been here before, and that's why I'm not afraid. Celest did say that the dreams I've been having are really memories.

And as insane as it sounds, I feel like this used to be my home. I can feel it coursing through me. But how can that be possible? I would remember a place as beautiful as this.

I'm just about to give up for the night and sleep under a tree until morning comes. I'm beginning to think I lost my mind. Maybe I have finally become so delusional that I wandered off and got myself lost. I can picture my mom freaking out with a search party out looking for me.

But then, what seemed to be out of nowhere, I see a clearing with the silhouette of a house. I run as fast as I can and pray that Vincent is there. I pray that these feelings are right and I'm not crazy. I get to the clearing in the woods, and it takes my breath away. Even in the dark, I can see its true beauty. It's a small house, maybe just enough for one or two people to live in. And it looks like it came straight from a medieval fairytale. There's a small barn to the right, with goats, cows, and sheep grazing lazily in the pasture, a wooden fence holding them in. Everything about this place feels like a different time.

I walk up to the house, reaching the front door. Hesitating, I tap lightly. No answer. I peer through the window, but I can't see much of anything. I know someone must live here because of the animals in the pasture. Maybe they're sleeping, or maybe they just aren't home. Either way, I don't feel comfortable just letting myself in.

I turn to head toward the barn. I would sleep there for the night and hope the owner wouldn't be too upset about it. I only make it a few steps before I hear a creaking sound behind me. I whirl around and see that the front door to the house is slowly opening.

"H-hello?" I call out, my voice shaking slightly.

Silence.

I cautiously step forward and walk inside, the wooden floorboards creaking under my weight. This is it. This is where I get lured to my death. I let out a sigh. *Oh, shut up, Ren. You're talking yourself into a tizzy.*

"Hello," I say again as I enter.

The room is dark, so I fumble around for a light switch, failing miserably. Realizing my phone is in my pocket, I take it out and switch the flashlight on. And I can't help but notice I have no service. Wherever I am, I'm far off the beaten path.

Right in front of me is an old wooden table with a few candles and matches. I quickly light them, and the whole room becomes bright. I'm just as amazed with the inside as I am the outside. The house is small, yet cozy. It has the same medieval feel to it. A small wooden table, with two wooden chairs lie positioned in the middle of the room. To the right, is a fireplace with a black pot hanging over it. To the left, are shelves lining the wall with spices in clear, glass jars. In the far corner by the fireplace is a bed, all made up and tidy with a quilt sprawled over it. That's the extent of it. No bathroom. No plumbing or electricity. No kitchen. Just one small room. Oddly though, it felt more like my home than my own.

I decide there could be no harm in staying here for a while. If someone showed up, I'd apologize and say I thought it was vacant. If I had to, I'd tell a sad story of being lost. That it was getting dark, and I needed a place to stay. None of it was a lie.

I sit at the table for a while, staring at the candles as the flames danced. They were relaxing and tranquil. The flickering light creates dancing shadows on the walls, adding to the room's cozy ambiance. So much so, that I feel like I can't keep my eyes open any longer.

I stand so I wouldn't fall asleep. I needed to stay awake in case whoever lived here returned home. As the night goes on, it becomes colder. I shiver as I rub my arms and walk over to the fireplace. I put a couple of small logs on and try to light the fire to no avail. I strike match after match, watching the small flame dance on the end of the stick, only to have it burn out when I toss it in the fireplace.

"Damn it!" I say as I strike another match.

This time, the flame grows larger as I put it under the logs. Finally! I grab a couple more pieces of kindling to put on the fire, and when I turn around, the fire is out again. Just a small line of smoke rising from the wood, eventually fading.

I let out a loud, irritated sigh as I throw the kindling to the ground.

"Light, damnit!" I yell.

Suddenly, a big burst of flames comes up from under the wood. It crackles and bounces happily as if it had been lit for hours. I jump back, startled as I look around the room and then back to the fire.

"How the hell...?" I ask myself as I look around the room again. I don't know what I expect to see exactly. But I also don't know how the fire lit itself. "It's okay, Serenity. It's just the heat from all those matches," I try telling myself. But in my gut, I feel that it's something more. Fires don't just light themselves.

I shake my head, slowly walking away from the fire, glancing back a few times as if it were somehow alive. The flickering flames cast a warm, inviting glow over the room, making it feel even more like home.

I finally decide that I can't stay awake any longer. My eyelids feel too heavy to keep open. It's been too much day for me to handle. Not wanting to go in the barn, I glance at the bed. It seems as though it is calling my name.

"I suppose it wouldn't hurt to just..." I plop down on the bed, sinking into the soft mattress and the warmth of the quilt. The comfort envelops me, and I fall instantly asleep, feeling a sense of peace and belonging that I've never felt before.

Chapter 12

The morning sun peered through the tall, stained-glass windows, casting vibrant patterns on the stone floor. Below, the bustling village was alive with activity. Men tilled the fields, their strong arms working rhythmically to plant seeds for the winter crop. Women were busy with outside chores, tidying their homes and tending to gardens, while children filled the crisp morning air with their carefree laughter, chasing each other through the narrow cobblestone streets.

As I stood at the windows, watching them all, a tinge of jealousy crept into my heart. Though their lives were undoubtedly difficult, they had a sense of peace. Peace was something I had never found with Celest as my mother. Recently, I had found a small sense of security with Vincent, but with that security came fear. Being madly in love with a man Celest so deeply despised brought great risk. She had threatened harm to both of us, and I knew she would be more than willing to make good on those threats if it suited her.

Despite the threats, I couldn't stay away from Vincent, no matter how hard I tried. There was a strong force pulling us together from the moment we laid eyes on each other, and that feeling only grew stronger each time I saw him. I knew magic must be part of it, but I didn't know how or why. Why just between us?

Ancient and powerful magic existed in our realm and had since the beginning of time, but I had never known of magic that drew two people so close together, making them feel more powerful when they were together. Though I possessed some magical abilities myself, I wasn't a powerful sorceress. I was limited to smaller things—making fire with my hands, moving objects with my mind. But I had never been able to wield any magical weapons or cast any spells.

After that first kiss with Vincent in the stables, I felt a power growing within me that I had never felt before. The power that possessed me when I was with him was unlike any magical force I knew to exist.

I clasped my hands together, trying to ease the tingling sensation, when another feeling washed over me. I felt a warm current coursing through my body, and I knew instantly what it was, for I had felt it many times before. I quickly glanced over to the courtyard, scanning across the knights until finally, my eyes landed on Vincent. He must have felt it too because his sword nearly slipped from his hand as he looked up at me, our eyes locking with such force it nearly took the breath from my lungs.

He smiled warmly as he continued to watch me through the window. I instinctively touched my hand to the glass as if to reach out to him. What was this incredible feeling? This man was my whole world, and I had only known him for a short time.

The knight he's practicing with becomes curious as his gaze follows Vincent's until it reaches me. A cocky smile spread across his face as he looks back at Vincent, nudging him teasingly. I quickly take my hand off the glass, embarrassed, as Vincent smiles up at me one more time before getting back to work.

My mind slips back to the night of our first kiss. A fire lit within my soul, quite literally, and the same happened to Vincent. Since then, we have been inseparable. We usually sneak away to go for a ride on the horses or a short walk down the trail. Often, while walking through the village, I would find myself being swept into a secluded alley by his loving arms, just so he could steal a kiss.

I knew what we were doing was reckless and dangerous, but something inside of me screamed to be with him. And once by his side, only then did the screaming stop. Besides, I was sure Celest didn't know. If she did, she would have done something about it by now.

I shiver at the thought of it. If she were to do something to Vincent, I'm not sure what I would do. But killing Celest has crossed my mind more times than I'd care to admit. It was becoming increasingly clear to me that something needed to be done about her. Though Celest was immortal, there had to be a way to knock her down just long enough to finally be free of her. There were plenty of those much more powerful than Celest. Could I get an ancient sorcerer on my side? One who would be willing to overthrow a queen?

If we failed, the results would be treacherous. Especially for me, if she ever found out I was behind it all. Not so much for my well-being, but for Vincent. The thought of what Celest might do to him made my stomach turn to knots.

I shake my head, trying to clear my thoughts. I don't have time to plan a treasonous act now. For now, I have to see Uncle Edmond. I hadn't seen him since the incident that night with Celest in his chambers. He had taken off the next day on a quest to find more young knights for our army. He had been gone for two weeks, and I was beginning to fear he would never return. But to my relief, he came riding in early this morning, empty-handed. There were no new men at his side, which I found odd. There were always those willing to protect the realm.

I look down to Vincent one more time before leaving. He was wielding his sword flawlessly, sweat dripping down his forehead and glistening in the sun. I want more than anything to go down there and kiss him for the whole world to see. To claim him as mine. But I quickly thought better of it.

As I turn to leave, I catch a glimpse of two guards marching towards him. I stop breathing as I watch, waiting to see who they were coming for. Bile rises in my throat as I see them stop right in front of

Vincent. They say a few words to him before grabbing him by both arms, dragging him away.

"No!" I yell as I pound on the glass. "No! What are you doing with him?"

"Ren," I hear Uncle Edmond say behind me.

I whirl around to see he too is being dragged by two guards, heading straight for the throne room. The blood in my veins turns to ice as I realize what is happening. Uncle and Vincent are being arrested. And Celest held no prisoners for long.

"What the hell do you think you're doing?" I ask, getting in the guard's face, stopping him in his tracks. "I demand you let him go immediately!"

"Sorry, miss. By orders of the queen," is all the guard says before brushing past me.

"Uncle!" I call out, feeling hopeless now.

"Ren, it's all going to be okay," he assures me. "Just stay out here."

I completely ignore his request. I will be damned if I sat out here and waited to find out what their fate would be. Though I already knew.

We reach the doors to the throne room, and they fling open. Celest sits high and mighty on her throne, her crown sitting proudly atop her head. The look on her face forces the contents of my stomach to my throat, and I force myself to choke it back. As we make our way to Celest, a row of guards and noblemen stand on either side of us. I know there would be no means of escape.

We stand directly in front of Celest now, and the guards throw Uncle Edmond to the ground at her feet. I give them a cold glare before reaching down, helping Uncle to his knees. As he looks up at me, my heart breaks with the sadness that fills his eyes.

"It's okay, sweetheart. Just wait outside," he says.

I shake my head. "No, uncle. I'm not leaving you alone with her," I say as I touch his sweat-stained face. He closes his eyes briefly as he forces a smile.

"Serenity, darling! I'm so glad you're here. I can't wait for you to witness this!" Celest says with a wicked smile.

I glare up at her, and it takes everything I have not to jump on her. Thoughts of taking her life crosses my mind for the millionth time today, and I quickly shake them away. Killing her was impossible, and it would only prove worse for Uncle and Vincent.

"What is this all about, Celest?" I ask in a threatening tone.

Celest holds up a hand. "Patience, my dear. We still have one more guest coming! He should be here any moment now."

Just as she finishes speaking, the doors fly open once more. I quickly turn to see Vincent being dragged towards us. We lock eyes as he is slammed down to his knees next to Uncle. He looks up at me, fearful, and I can feel the blood draining from my face. I cup his cheek in my hand momentarily, shock waves crashing through me as I do, before turning back to Celest.

"What the hell is all of this?" I ask, stepping closer to her. I quickly have guards in my face, blocking me from drawing too close to my wretched mother.

"Move. Now," I warn them as I inch closer until I'm nose to nose with one of them. I can feel his breath creeping down my cheeks, and it makes me want to vomit.

They quickly place their hands on their swords, ready to strike me down. I don't move though. They would have to strike me down if they were to get to Uncle and Vincent.

"It's alright," Celest says to the guards, and they quickly move out of the way. I am now face to face with her, the wicked smile still present on her expression.

"Such a brave little mouse," Celest says before pushing me out of the way so she could see her prisoners.

"Sir Edmond, Sir Vincent, I hereby find you guilty of treason," Celest says as she glances between them, looking all too proud of herself.

My blood begins to boil as rage nestles itself deep in my soul. "This is absurd! Under what grounds?" I ask as I step directly in front of her again.

"Your beloved uncle conspired against me. Didn't you Sir Edmond?" She says as she looks at uncle.

"You're damn right I did. And I'd do it again in a minute," uncle says through gritted teeth.

"Uncle, what is she talking about?" I ask.

"Focus, Serenity," Celest says as she snaps her fingers. "He also challenged his queen. You

remember. You were there," she says, referring to the night she caught uncle and I talking about Vincent. That was when it all began. And now I have even more questions. Why did uncle leave the next day if not to find more knights? And what conspiracy did he commit against Celest? Was it about Vincent?

"He's your brother, you wench!" I yell.

Celest narrows her eyes at me before turning to Vincent. "Sir Vincent also conspired against me. He refuses to stop seeing you, even though I forbade it."

"What are you talking about? We haven't been seeing each other!" I lie. I wasn't about to admit it to her.

Celest lets out a bone chilling laugh, sending chills down my spine. "Oh, my dear. You don't think mommy is that stupid, do you?" She quickly grabs my wrist, and I wince in pain. "Did you think you could hide this from me?" She asks as she yanks up my sleeve, revealing the delicate ink on my forearm. "I'd wager your dear, sweet Vincent has the same one.

I say nothing as I glare at her with threatening eyes. My heart pounds fiercely as we stand there for a moment, challenging each other. Celest continues. "I have had you fallowed for weeks now. It seems you two have been spending quite a lot of time together. Ah, young love!" She exclaims as she places her hand over her heart.

The same heart I'm dying to rip out of her chest.

"I was going to arrest him that first day. But I thought I'd wait for my brother's return. It's so much more dramatic this way, don't you think? And I so can't wait to see the look on my poor daughter's face when I deliver the news."

"Spit it out, Celest," I say, my knees feeling weak now.

Celest gives a happy smile as she looks to me, and then turning to uncle and Vincent. "Do you two have any last words?" Celest asks, looking between the two of them.

"Yeah, actually," Vincent says.

"Go on..." Celest presses.

"I love Serenity. I have from the moment our eyes met that first day. And nothing you ever say or do will change that. Go ahead and kill me. Because not being with her would be a far worse fate than death ever could be," he says, looking up to me now, tears filling his eyes.

I drop down to my knees next to him and place my hands on either side of his cheeks. "I love you, Vincent," I say as I kiss him deeply, sending an explosion to my core. I know this will only deepen Celest's anger, and she'll probably have me locked away until the end of time. But I don't care. I have to feel his lips pressed against mine before it was too late.

"Well, isn't this adorable!" Celest cheers. She turns to uncle now. "Sir Edmond, any last words?"

Uncle looks between Vincent and I, and then back to Celest. "Burn in hell, bitch."

Celest's face floods with anger as she stands. "Sir Edmond, Sir Vincent, I hear by sentence you to die by beheading. Your execution will be now."

Did she just say…now? My head spins as I try to grasp what she just said. I knew it would happen, but I never expected her to say it would be happening now. I had planned out in my head how I would help them escape before the execution took place. But now…

Before I can form another thought, a rage deeper than I've ever felt before crashes through me with such force it takes my breath away. I begin to notice an intense, burning vibration on my arm where the ink is. Vincent must feel it too, because he winces as he glances down at his own arm. A powerful sensation sweeps over my body, and I suddenly feel invincible.

I look over to Vincent, and we lock eyes. He's staring at me with as much power as I'm feeling, and he nods his head once. Somehow, I know exactly what he means, and I nod back. Before I can make a move, Vincent breaks free of his chains with such force I almost jump. But the strong presence of the power within me holds me steady as I turn to Celest.

I throw my hands up to her, the power that's been begging to come out finally does. It shatters the windows with such force, it echoes through every hallway in the castle. Celest flies backwards, hitting the wall behind her, knocking her unconscious. The guards immediately draw their swords, the sharp tips pointed at my chest.

I sigh in frustration. "You really don't want to get in my way," I say. But they don't back down.

"Fine," I say as I throw my hands up to them, sending them flying across the room. More guards surround uncle and Vincent now, their swords to their throats, ready to kill.

"Now that is a really bad idea," I say.

Vincent grabs the blade that's pressed to his neck, pushing it away from him with ease. Not a single drop of blood is spilled from his hand. He quickly turns, pushing the sword in to the guard's stomach as I flick my wrist, snapping the neck of the guard who held Uncle Edmond.

"Where did you learn to do that?" Uncle asks in astonishment as he looks between Vincent and me.

"I have no idea," we say in unison.

I have never been able to possess such powerful magic before. It's as though the rage I felt inside of me awakened a power I never knew existed.

"I think I just fell even more in love with you," Vincent says as he looks around at the guards I sent flying. I smile at him as I go over to untie uncle.

I go over to Vincent now and kiss him deeply. The ink on our arms comes to life once more, stopping us. This time, the delicate oak tree is glowing with life on both of us.

"That's incredible," uncle says in awe.

"What's happening to us," I ask him. I get the feeling he knows something by the way he's watching us.

"How should I know?" He asks as he shifts his body, clearly lying. "We have to get out of here. It's not safe to stay here anymore."

"Where will we go?" Vincent asks.

I purse my lips together. Of all the times I dreamed of escaping this place, I never thought of where I would actually go.

"I know of a place," uncle says. "Come. We haven't much time."

Chapter 13

We run as fast as we can to the stables to gather the horses. The urgency in the air is palpable, and my heart races with every step. I am just about to mount when a sudden realization hits me like a bolt of lightning.

"Wait! We have to go back for Arian!" I shout, my voice trembling with panic.

"Love, we haven't the time. Celest will be coming for us at any moment. We'll come back for her. I promise," Vincent says as he cups my face in his hands, his touch warm and reassuring despite the urgency.

"I can't just leave her!" I cry, my voice breaking.

"We have to go, sweetheart. Right now," Uncle Edmond says sternly, his eyes filled with a mixture of fear and determination.

My panic is interrupted as the warning bells begin to ring, their sound echoing through the night, signaling that Celest is now awake and searching for us. A new kind of terror grips me as we quickly mount our horses, the urgency of the situation sinking in.

We take off past the gates and into the village. People screech and hurriedly move out of the way as we storm past them. Normally, I would be more careful in a busy street full of people, but now I couldn't care less. We need to hide ourselves before it is too late.

Once we reach the forest, we begin to pick up speed. The cool wind whips against my face, and I don't bother to look back at the place I've always called home. It isn't anymore, and I never care to see it again.

As we ride deeper into the forest, the sounds of the village fade away, replaced by the rustling of leaves and the distant calls of nocturnal creatures. The forest is dense, the trees towering above us, their branches intertwining to form a canopy that blocks out the moonlight. The ground is covered in a thick carpet of leaves, and the air is filled with the earthy scent of moss and damp wood.

"We should be there by nightfall," Uncle Edmond says as we begin to slow our pace, his voice a calm anchor in the chaos.

"Where, exactly?" I ask, my curiosity and fear battling for dominance.

"You'll see soon," he replies, his tone cryptic, which only puts me more on edge. What does he know that we don't?

We reach the clearing where Vincent and I first spent time together. I smile warmly as I think back to that day. It was the first time we knew that there was something special between us as we touched. The curiosity settled its way into my heart, and so did Vincent. Little did I know then; our bond would become even more curious, leaving me with a thousand questions.

And little did I know then, that even though it was a fond memory, it was also the beginning of a nightmare. Yet, even if I did know then what I know now, I don't think I could have prevented it even if I tried. There was a strong force pulling us together. No willpower in the world was as strong as our undying need to be together. Even though I should, I don't regret a thing. Especially throwing Celest against the wall. I can still hear the sound of her head cracking, and it brings another warm smile to my face. I've been wanting to do that for so long, and I finally possessed the power to do it. How I have that much power, I don't know. I've had a sense of strong magic brewing in me since the night Vincent and I kissed. How is it possible that one simple kiss could do that? But it wasn't just a kiss. It was something much, much more. Something shifted inside of me that night, changing my life forever.

"What's that?" Vincent asks, snapping me from my thoughts.

"Where?" I ask as I begin to look around, my heart beginning to thud with anticipation.

"There, by the water," he says, pointing to the pond.

"It looks like a person," Uncle Edmond says. "Let's check it out. But brace yourselves."

We carefully make our way to the other side of the pond, preparing to fight if we have to. I fear more than anything that Celest made her way here before we did, waiting to strike. This time, it wouldn't be as easy to defeat her now that she's been alerted about how powerful I have become. She'll be ready this time.

"Ren!" I hear a familiar voice calling my name as a girl stands from the grass.

"Arian?" I squeal as I jump from my horse, running to her and hugging her tight. "Arian, what on earth are you doing out here?"

She studies my eyes carefully. "You wouldn't believe me if I told you."

"Try me," I press, my curiosity piqued.

"Well, I…I had a dream last night. I dreamt that your uncle, Sir Edmond, and Sir Vincent were arrested. Someone came to me, Ren. He said I needed to go to this pond to wait for you and that you'd be along soon."

The breath catches in my lungs. "How…?"

Arian shakes her head, looking puzzled. "I'm sure it was nothing. They obviously haven't been arrested if they're here with you now," she says, looking between them.

"No. They were arrested. Just a while ago. We escaped."

"W-what?" Arian stammers. "How was I able to see it before it happened?"

"I've heard of this before," Uncle Edmond chimes in, his voice thoughtful. "She's a soothsayer."

"A…what?" Arian asks cautiously.

"You can foretell the future. Sometimes through dreams, other times through visions."

Arian's face pales as she stares at Uncle Edmond. "I've never been able to do this before. Why now?" she asks, her voice trembling.

"I'm not sure. It's suspicious that it should begin now. But I have a feeling it was for a very important purpose."

"I can't wrap my head around any of this," Arian says as she paces, her eyes scanning the ground, her mind clearly racing.

I put a hand on her shoulder, trying to steady her from her racing thoughts. "We'll figure this out. I promise. But for now, we have to be going. You can ride with me," I say, offering her a reassuring smile.

Arian calms a little as she nods. I quickly jump back on Juniper and offer her my hand as she climbs up behind me. Her grip is firm, and I can feel her shaking slightly.

"Lead the way, Uncle," I say as we head out once more, the forest closing in around us, offering a sense of protection as we delve deeper into its embrace.

Chapter 14

The journey is long and arduous, the path winding through dense thickets and over rocky terrain. The sounds of the forest are both soothing and eerie, the rustling leaves whispering secrets in the wind. My mind races with thoughts of what lies ahead, the uncertainty gnawing at me.

Nightfall is quickly approaching as the sun sinks low beneath the trees. I shiver as the cool air wraps itself snugly around my body. The trees sway eerily in the breeze, their shadows bouncing off the ground like restless spirits. We've been riding for hours, and my back begins to ache with built-up tension. Though I'm feeling on edge, exhaustion settles into my bones. I nod off a few times, only to be jolted awake by Juniper's bobbing movements. I glance back at Arian, and she's fast asleep with her head resting on my back. I can't help but smile; the peace spread across her face makes me feel a little less nervous.

Vincent rides up next to me, gently placing his hand on mine. "How are you doing, love?" he asks, his eyes gently peering into mine.

My knees begin to weaken at his touch. I will never get used to the vibrating current I feel on my skin every time he's near. "I'm doing okay," I say with a smile.

He rubs my hand with his thumb. "Liar," he teases.

I let out a small laugh. "Well, I am a little tired," I admit.

"You look exhausted," he points out, concern evident in his voice.

I let out a long sigh. "I am," I admit, though I didn't want to admit it even to myself. Being tired meant being weak. And being weak left me vulnerable to my enemies.

I shiver at the thought. What if we're being followed? It couldn't be that hard to pick up our trail. We aren't too far off any main path. I look around now, feeling paranoid.

"I'll never let anything happen to you, Ren," he says, sensing my fear.

"And I'll never let anything happen to you. Not ever," I say, gently squeezing his hand.

"You proved that today," he says with a smile, his lips curving perfectly, revealing his blinding white teeth. I instinctively bite my lip as my eyes travel from his lips to his eyes. Vincent raises a brow, giving me a devilish grin.

He laces his fingers between mine and looks at me with such a burning desire, I can feel my face turning red. "I want to kiss every inch of your body, Serenity," he says in a low voice.

My heart flutters in my chest, my breath quickly catching in my throat. "Please do," I breathe.

"Ugh, gross," Arian says as she stirs awake.

"Shut up, Arian," I say teasingly, a small grin playing at my lips.

"Now, now children. Be nice to each other," Uncle Edmond says with a chuckle. "We're here."

I quickly glance up and can't believe my eyes. There, in the middle of the forest, are two long rows of trees. Their branches overlap one another, creating a thick, green canopy. The entrance is covered with a lush curtain of vines.

"Uncle, what is this place?" I ask in awe.

"It's called the Valley of The Warriors," he says, staring up at it with as much amazement as I feel.

"How have I never heard of this place? Or seen this place?" I ask. I've been through this part of the forest a hundred times in my life and have never noticed it before.

"Because it's always been a well-kept secret guarded by magic. Your…I, uh, a friend of mine created it. It's a sort of safe haven," Uncle stammers.

I narrow my eyes at him. He isn't being entirely truthful. I've never known him to lie to me before, so why now? What could he possibly be protecting?

"Shall we get settled in and get some rest?" Vincent suggests.

"Yes, let's," Uncle quickly responds, breaking the staring match between us.

We dismount the horses and stretch out the aching in our muscles from the long ride. Uncle is the first to enter through the thick curtain, holding it open and ushering us inside. As I draw closer, I can feel the magic radiating off and into my bones. It feels so familiar…so inviting. Though I know I've never felt magic like it before. But it seemed my soul does as it urges me to move closer until I'm finally standing inside.

What I see causes my breath to falter. Beautiful is an understatement. What I'm seeing is a completely different world with tall, bowing trees with thick, green leaves stretching down almost to the ground. The ground itself is covered in soft, vibrant green moss. Looking up proves to be just as stunning. Though the sun is setting, it shines brightly with a magical glow. Despite that, stars fill the sky, twinkling proudly together. A crescent moon on the opposite side of the sun. To the far end, there is a mystical waterfall, flowing lazily into a pool of clear, blue water. Rocks covered in moss scatter along its edges. The beauty seems to stretch on for as far as I can see as I continue to scan the area.

"Wow," Arian says as she spins in circles, taking in the beauty.

"Someone created this?" I ask in astonishment.

"Yes. It's beautiful, isn't it?" Uncle says with a smile. His eyes warm as they watch me.

"It's astonishing," I say, breathless.

"We were hoping you'd be pleased," he says.

"We?" I ask, snapping my head towards him once more.

"Did I say we? I meant me. I am glad you like it," Uncle says, shifting uncomfortably in place.

I raise a brow at him as I fold my arms across my chest. "Uncle, if I didn't know any better, I'd say you're hiding something from me."

"Nonsense, Ren," he scoffs. "Now, let's get settled in and have a bite to eat. You all must be starving!"

He stomps away before I can get another word in, and it only adds to my growing curiosity. He is hiding something. And I need to find out what.

We follow Uncle to the center of the valley where a fire is already lit, with fish grilling to perfection over the flames.

"Where did the food come from?" I ask, the scent making my mouth water.

"You're just full of questions today," Uncle teases. "This place was designed to fully protect and live in until it's safe to return to the outside world. Everything you could ever need is here."

I want to ask how he knows all of this, but I decide better of it. He wouldn't give me a straight answer anyway.

The four of us sit quietly by the fire as we scrounge up every last bit of fish off our plates, while the horses drink lazily from the pool of water. By the time we're finished, I'm so tired I can hardly keep my eyelids from closing.

I'm brought back to reality as I feel the familiar buzzing on my skin. I glance over to see Vincent has clasped my hand, watching me with soft eyes.

"You're exhausted," he points out.

"That I am. I don't think I could stay awake any longer if I tried."

"It's been a long day. Why don't we all get some rest?" Uncle suggests.

"Where do we sleep?" I ask.

"In the huts, of course," Uncle says, nodding his head behind me.

Under the swooping trees are small, yet elegant huts aligned in a row. The curtains are opened just enough for me to see a big bed covered in over-sized blankets and fluffy pillows, a soft light illuminating from inside. I sigh in contentment as I picture myself plopping onto the bed, falling fast asleep.

I quickly stand, accepting the warm invitation of the hut.

"I trust you'll look after my niece tonight?" Uncle asks Vincent. "The valley is mostly intangible, but I'd sleep better knowing I don't have to worry."

"Yes, sir. Of course, I will," Vincent says as he looks at me with passion filling his eyes.

I smile up at him before walking to the hut I chose for myself. I look back at him as he tends to the horses, watching his muscles shift perfectly with every movement, before stepping through the thin curtain of the trees and into the hut.

I plop down on the giant bed, letting the blankets wrap themselves around me tightly, and I sigh. I've never felt anything more comfortable, more magical in my life. I savor the moment for as long as I can, for I know this pleasant feeling won't be lasting forever. A war hangs in the balance. I can feel

Celest's rage pounding in my heart, and I know she'll stop at nothing to find me. She would never just let me leave the castle, never to return. And she most certainly wouldn't allow Uncle and Vincent to escape unscathed. She needed to have her revenge.

But for tonight, I vow to myself not to think about it. I need this one blissful moment before Celest's rage is unleashed.

"Can I come in for a moment?" Vincent asks. He's standing in the small opening to the hut, leaning against its side, a small grin playing at his lips. No doubt from the way I have myself cocooned in the blankets.

"Of course, you can," I say as I sit up.

"I just wanted to say goodnight," he says as he lingers near the bed.

I can't help but to smile at his hesitation. I tap the bed lightly, inviting him over. "I'm glad you did," I say as he sits next to me. Vibrations course through my body with intense force as he draws closer to me.

He pauses for a moment. "Do you feel that?"

"I do. A sort of vibration?"

"Exactly," he says, nodding his head. "What do you suppose it means?"

"I don't know," I say thoughtfully. "All I know is it grew stronger after we kissed. My powers have too."

He nods in agreement as he gently grabs my hand, tracing his thumb over the ink on my forearm.

"These must be part of...whatever is happening," he says.

"Maybe it means we were made for each other," I say teasingly. But deep down I really do wonder if that's the true meaning behind the tattoos we share.

He becomes serious, his eyes searing into mine with intense passion. "Gods, I hope so," he says in a low tone.

My heart quickens at his words as my skin begins to flush. I reach up, caressing his cheek with the back of my hand. He lets out a satisfied sigh as he closes his eyes, reaching up to wrap his hand around the nape of my neck.

"Vincent..." I say in a whisper. The sound of his name coming from my lips makes his grip tighten around me.

Before he can respond, I press my lips against his. The undeniable current crashing through me with such force, it makes my head spin. We move our mouths together faster now and with urgency. He explores down to my neck until finally reaching my collar bone, leaving a searing hot trail as his tongue brushes against my skin. I let a moan escape as I push myself harder against him, craving every inch of his body.

I'm just about to tear his clothes off when a command, echoing deep within my mind, urges me to stop. He must have heard...or felt it too, for we break away from each other at the same time, heaving for breath.

"I assume you felt that too," I ask breathlessly.

He only nods, his forehead resting against mine as he trembles with overflowing excitement. I reach up, tracing the back of his ear, down to his neck. "I don't think I can stop," I whisper.

He lets out a husky moan as he crashes his lips against mine. The hunger of needing him drives me to madness and I push him down to the bed. I quickly straddle him as I nibble the lobe of his ear and down to his neck where I softly latch on with my teeth. I can feel the excitement coursing through him just as it is me.

He grabs my waist, flipping me over onto my back as he hovers directly over me. "You're my own personal drug, Ren. I can never get enough of you," he says in a husky tone.

"Then don't stop," I urge. "I need all of you, Vincent. And I need you inside of me before I go completely mad."

My words drive him crazy as he teases me, his hard member pressed firmly against me. I curse the fact that our clothes are still on as I reach down to grab him, his member completely filling my hand. He reaches his hand under my skirt, tracing his fingertips along my inner thighs until he finds the exact spot I need him to be. The friction of his fingers penetrating me sends me over the edge as I fall into a sea of oblivion. I quickly undo his pants, urgent to get a better feel of his member. I grip him firmly, moving my hand in soft strokes as he traces his lips across my chest, his hands still hard at work. He lifts my skirt up further, his member now touching my inner thigh as he stares into my eyes, brushing the hair from my face.

"Are you sure?" he whispers.

"Yes," I breathe. "Yes. Please."

I reach down to guide him inside of me, almost forgetting about the urgent command not to do this.

"No. You need to stop. Now. It isn't the right time," a loud voice echoes.

Vincent and I stop as we glance around. No one is with us, yet somehow, we both heard the voice as if they were standing right next to us.

"What the hell was that?" Vincent asks as he scans the room.

I take a few deep breaths, trying to regain my composure. "I...I don't know."

He clears his throat as he rests his forehead on mine, his sweet breath playing at my lips. "It really doesn't want this to happen right now, does it?"

I reach up, caressing his sweat-stained cheek. "I guess not. I could almost feel its...urgency."

"So could I," he says.

I let out a frustrated sigh as I groan. Vincent gives a cocky grin.

"Are you whining?" he asks teasingly.

"Yes," I say with a pout.

He lets out a laugh as he kisses my forehead. "It seems you crave me as much as I do you."

"You have no idea," I say, willing myself the power to refrain from devouring him.

He rolls off me now as he zips his pants back up. He props up on his elbow as he stares down at me, his gaze making my body hot all over again. "I felt something else," he says. "It'll happen when it's supposed to. It wasn't saying no forever."

I nod my head, knowing he's right. Whatever force it was telling us to stay apart wasn't doing so maliciously. And I could feel that it would happen when the time is right. Right for what, I can't begin to guess.

"I felt that too," I say as I place my hand on his chest.

He reaches over, his lips just barely grazing my ear. "When the time comes, Serenity, I'm going to make you feel like you've never felt before," he whispers.

I shiver with excitement. The thought of what we would feel when the time does come brings a wave of heat to my cheeks. When we first kissed, an intense power ignited within us, setting our souls ablaze. I couldn't imagine what actually being with him would bring. And I can't wait to find out.

We lie under the blankets together, his arm wrapped tightly around me. I place my hand on his chest and kiss it softly before closing my eyes. The sweet scent of his musk washes over me, sending me into a state of deep tranquility. Nothing else in the world matters in this moment. For every moment with him is eternal bliss.

Chapter 15

My eyes spring open as I struggle to catch my breath. I look around, feeling confused and panicked. The cottage surrounding me is entirely unfamiliar. I rub my eyes with force, and that's when I finally remember I stepped through the giant, glowing ball and ended up in this peculiar place. I have no idea if I'm still in Maine, a different state, or an entirely different country altogether.

I sit up in the bed, going over the events of the dream I just had. I can still feel the excitement in my core as I fondly remember Vincent's hands on me...and in me. It was by far the most erotic moment of my life, even if it was just a dream. And all that power. I rub my hands together, feeling an intense tingling in my fingertips. Surely, magic couldn't be real. The thought of it alone is absurd. But how else could I explain everything that's happened? How is it possible for anyone to step through a glowing ball and end up somewhere different? The only explanation that sounds even remotely plausible is magic, as crazy as it is.

Was that how the fire lit last night?

I jump from the bed and stare down at the fireplace, hot coals still smoldering. I glance around to make sure no one is watching me before turning back to the coals.

"Light!" I say sternly as I hold my hands out to it.

Nothing.

I let out a huff as I try it again. And again. But still, there is no flame bouncing to life. I shake my head, feeling like an idiot. Obviously, I don't have magic like my dream suggested. So, if that part of it wasn't real, was any of it? My heart sinks as I get the strong urge to fall to my knees. The very thought of Vincent not being real sends me into a grief-stricken state. I need him to be real. And Arian and Uncle Edmond. I love them all with all my heart. Especially Vincent. There's something so special about him. So special about us together. I can still feel the intenseness of his touch coursing through my veins…

A rooster crows right outside the window, making me jump, reminding me that I haven't eaten in nearly two days. Suddenly, I'm starving. I make the decision to gather a couple of eggs to cook up. I'm sure whoever owns this place will understand. I hope anyway. And after, I'll be on my way again, as if I were never here to begin with.

Where I would go, or what direction I would head in, I have no idea. But something within me has led me this far, almost as though it was pushing me forward, straight to this cottage. Images of the dream flash through my mind again. The feeling was eerily similar to the feeling Vincent and I had when we were urged not to share our bodies with one another. Was it the same person or thing telling me where to go now? I shake my head, thinking better of it. How could it be the same?

I let out a sigh, feeling defeated. So far, whatever it was, seemed misguiding. It brought me here to this empty place, no real answers to be had. It's likely if I keep going, I'll become even more lost than I already am. But I know I have to keep going. I need to find out what's happening and to find the answers which I so desperately seek. Even if I am losing my grip on reality, I need to know that for sure. And then maybe I can find the help I need and move on with my life.

My stomach grumbles again, urging me towards the door. I assume the chicken coop must be somewhere near the barn, so I'll start there. If not, I'll eat a chicken. I don't care at this point.

I turn the handle on the door, pushing it open. At the same time, someone is pulling it open from the other side. I stumble directly into the person, my face smashing into his hard chest. And that's when I feel it. The buzzing. The strong current coursing through me like I've felt so many times before in my dreams. But this time it's stronger. More alive, more powerful.

My heart begins to pound fiercely in my chest as I fling my head up to look at the person. And…it's him. The man I've seen so many times before. The man I wasn't sure even existed.

It's Vincent.

"Oh, my God," I say in a shaky breath. He's real. And he's standing directly in front of me, looking sinfully handsome. His dark hair is tousled, falling slightly over his forehead, and his piercing green eyes lock onto mine with an intensity that sends shivers down my spine. His strong jawline is covered in a light stubble, adding to his rugged appeal.

"Ren..." He trails off as he drops his belongings to the floor. He's in complete shock as he stares into my eyes in the same loving manner I've grown used to. A single tear slips from his eye and down his cheek. He slowly reaches up, caressing my face, our skin vibrating together in perfect rhythm.

He lets out an excited breath. "Oh, my God. Serenity. It's really you!"

In one quick motion, he scoops me up into his strong arms. I wrap my arms tightly around his neck as I nuzzle into him. He feels even better against me in person. The dreams dulled what his touch really feels like. The current vibrating through me is so much stronger and more alive than I could have ever imagined.

"Vincent," I sigh into his ear, my voice trembling with emotion.

He gently pulls away to look at me again, but still holding me close. "It actually worked," he says in astonishment. "Your uncle and I finally found the right spell."

"A spell? Brought me back? To where exactly?" I ask as I look around the room. Though the familiarity of this place is undeniable, I've never seen this place before in my life. And Vincent. I wanted so badly to believe that he was real, but I didn't see how it was possible. I was almost convinced that madness had slowly crept its way into my mind. I look back to Vincent who's watching me closely. "And you're real." As relief floods through me, a single tear slips down my cheek, and he quickly wipes it away.

"Ren, what do you remember?" he asks, deep concern crossing his expression.

"I remember being at my house and having dreams. There was a light. I stepped through it and ended up in the middle of the woods." I look down at my hands, feeling embarrassed. Saying it out loud sounds even more ridiculous than in my head.

Vincent grabs my trembling hands as if to soothe them. "How did you end up here?"

"Something inside of me told me to keep walking. It stopped once I got here," I say, shaking my head now. "Am I crazy?"

"No, love," he says in a soft voice. "Your uncle said this could happen. All of your memories should return to you soon, now that you're back."

"Remember what exactly?" I ask as I peer up into his bold and endearing eyes, feeling a mix of hope and confusion.

"Our life together. Before Celest cast a spell to banish you."

I rub my forehead, afraid that I might be stuck in another dream. Until Vincent touches my face again. The rush of power that washes through me is undeniably real.

"What?" I ask. "I remember everything about my life. My childhood. My parents. I don't remember anything about you or this place."

Vincent winces at the last part. Pain and sadness crossing his face, and I feel as if my heart will shatter into a million little pieces.

"Hey," I say in a soft tone. "I'm sorry. I didn't mean to sound so rude. I'm just so overwhelmed and so confused."

His expression softens as he gives a sad smile. "I know, love. I promise you'll remember everything soon."

He hugs me again, lightly brushing his lips against my shoulder. The hair on the nape of my neck stands at attention as sparks jolt through me. I let out an erotic gasp, remembering the latest dream I had of our time together in the hut.

"I've missed that feeling," he whispers, his lips grazing the lobe of my ear.

My breath is still caught in my throat as I try to speak. "Me too. I mean, I only remember it from a couple of dreams I've had. But, actually feeling it like this…" I trail off.

"Why don't I make us some breakfast and you can tell me about your dreams?" he asks, curiosity rising in his tone.

I smile as I remember our erotic moment from the last dream I had. It's as if he can sense my growing arousal because he gives that same devilish grin I've grown to love so much.

"I'd like that," I say, my voice barely above a whisper, feeling the intense connection between us deepening with every passing moment.

Chapter 16

I eat my breakfast in silence. Everything that has happened is far too overwhelming to take in all at once. Vincent is real. I have always felt that he somehow was. Or, always hoped. But logic always stepped in, crowding my mind with other explanations. But here I am, eating eggs and bacon with a man I didn't know but love so much.

I finish scraping the last bits of food off my plate as I stare up at Vincent. He's watching me intently while fidgeting with his spoon, his brow slightly furrowed. Becoming uncomfortable, I look down to my tingling hands, rubbing the sensation out of them like I've done so many times before. I know I have to start talking eventually, but what do I say? That the only part of my life I remember is one in which he never existed? I mentioned that part to him earlier, the pained look on his face felt like a punch in the gut. Or maybe I should tell him that I do remember him in a way. That I see him every night in my dreams, and somehow, even though I don't know him, I've fallen madly in love with him.

God, I'm so in love with this man. Even more so now that he's sitting right in front of me.

I let out a sigh. "Vincent, I don't understand any of this."

He smiles softly. "I know, love," he says as he reaches across the table to grab my hand. His touch is warm and reassuring, sending calming waves through my chaotic thoughts. "Ask me anything. Maybe it'll all start coming back to you as we talk about it."

I nod in agreement as I think carefully. I have so many questions racing through my mind, it's difficult to keep them all straight. The intensity of the situation, the reality of his presence, and the surreal nature of everything that's happened make it hard to focus on just one thought.

"Why don't I remember you, or this life? Why do I only remember the...other life?" My voice trembles slightly, the fear and confusion I feel now coming to the surface.

Is that what you'd call it? Is this place my real life, while the only one I remember is really my other life?

"Celest cast a banishing spell on you. But it was something much more than that. While banishing you should have been good enough, it wasn't for her. She made it so you'd be reborn again into a completely different dimension, forgetting all about your life here..." He trails off as anger flashes through his fierce eyes, and he grips my hand a little tighter, as if to say: "I'm never letting you go again." I want to relish in the moment, but confusion settles its way into my mind once more.

"A different dimension?" I ask, looking around the room. The reality of his words starts to sink in, making the unfamiliar surroundings feel even more surreal. "I'm in a different dimension?"

Vincent nods slowly. "Yes. Welcome to Mirgora," he says as he holds out his hands, gesturing around us.

I blink rapidly as I try to comprehend the fact that not only am I not in Maine anymore, but I'm also not even in the same dimension where the earth I know exists.

"What the fuck," I say as I massage my temples, the overwhelming truth sinking in like a heavy weight.

Vincent cocks his brow, a grin spreading across his lips. "I see your language has remained the same," he teases, trying to lighten the mood.

I ignore his statement. "Reborn? So, do I look different than I did before? Am I still the same person?" The questions tumble out, each one a desperate attempt to understand this new reality.

Vincent's eyes roam my body, looking first to my eyes and down to my lips where he lingers for a long moment, causing my face to burn hot. "No, you don't look any different. Your beauty still stuns me to my core," he says with a devilish grin. My stomach flutters in anticipation. I want to kiss him now, more than ever before. The pull he has on me is so much stronger than my dreams led on.

"You don't seem too different," he continues. "Maybe a little more shy than normal. Do you remember anything at all about this life?"

I nod. "I think so. I've had bits and pieces creep through in dreams. Though none of it makes much sense. You have always been in them. We met after you became a knight. And the attraction between us was...instant. Intense," I say the last part with a shudder of excitement in my tone. I look into his eyes now, passion filling me to my core. "Celest seemed afraid of us being together. She forbade it. And when I went against her, she arrested you and uncle. I used magic or something to stop her."

I decide to stop speaking. The words coming out of my mouth sound insane.

"It seems you remember most of the important bits," Vincent says thoughtfully, his voice steadying my racing heart.

"But why? Why just now?"

"Because your uncle and I finally found the right spell to reverse that of the banishing spell. The only way it would work is if you believed. You had to truly believe, then the light would appear. And seeing how you're here now, a part of you must have believed in me. In us," he says as he stands from his chair and kneels next to me, his hand gently caressing my face. I close my eyes as I sigh at the tender nature of his touch.

"Of course, I believed. Something inside of me screamed at me that you were real. Celest warned me not to cross through, but I had to. I had to see you," I say, grabbing his hand in mine.

His face hardens as he clenches his jaw. "Celest came to you?"

"Yes…She possessed my mom's body and came to me in the middle of the night."

He instinctively grips my hand tighter. "She knew what we were up to. She's gonna know that you're back, and she'll be coming for us."

"But why?" I ask. "What did we ever do so wrong besides fall in love with each other? What's so wrong with that?"

He shakes his head. "We never found out. We had a plan to banish her from here. It worked. But at the same time, she was casting a banishing spell on you," he says, anger crossing his face.

"What do we do?" I ask, suddenly feeling like I may vomit. The thought of an evil witch coming after me…after Vincent…

"The first thing we need to do is find your uncle. He's been trying to find a way to be rid of her for good. He never gave up on you, Ren. And neither have I."

"How is it that uncle is even still alive?" I ask. I couldn't be any more relieved to find that he is. But how? Is he immortal too? He was in his sixties or so in my dreams, and nearly three decades have passed since then. He must be well into his nineties by now.

"Time travels much differently here in Mirgora than it does in other dimensions. To us, you've been gone for two years," Vincent says, anger crossing his face once more. "If it had been twenty-eight years for me as it has for you, I fear I would have never survived it."

I don't bother to say anything more. The world around me feels like it's spinning out of control. It has only been two years here that I've been gone. How is that even possible? I remember an entire lifetime without Vincent, but really, I've only been gone from him for two years.

Instead of dwelling on it, I hug his neck tight. I can't help myself anymore. I need to be wrapped in his arms, feeling the warmth of his flesh against mine. Though I don't remember him, he feels like home. He's exactly where I need to be.

"I've missed you so much. I didn't even know if you were real, and the thought terrified me. I needed you to be real. And here you are," I say with a sigh of relief, my voice trembling with emotion.

He wraps his arms around me a little tighter, our bodies pressed together much in the same way as that night in the hut...

"We'll never be apart again. We will stop Celest. And we'll finally be together in peace," he whispers in my ear. His breath plays teasingly against my flesh, sending excited chills down my arms.

"You know what my last memory of us was?" I ask, feeling bold. I have never felt so bold before, except in my dreams. Maybe a part of the real me is starting to return.

"Tell me," he says in a husky tone, as if my touch has intoxicated him.

"The first night we spent together in the hut."

Vincent lets out an excited sigh as the passion from his body burns into mine with intense heat.

"I've played that moment over and over in my mind for the past two years," he says with a shy grin. "It was the best moment of my life up until now."

I was about to say we could recreate the memory, but my mouth wouldn't move as the ground around me began to spin with such speed, I thought I might faint.

"Ren? Ren, what's the matter?" Vincent asks, panic rising in his voice. He grips my arms, trying to steady me as the world tilts precariously.

I try desperately to respond. But the feelings rushing through me are too intense. I can see that I'm falling to the ground as the world around me begins to tilt, but I can't feel it. The sensation is surreal, like a slow-motion descent into darkness. Before I could fall much further, Vincent catches me and gently lays me on the bed

Chapter 17

"Vincent, I've got it!" I say as I walk through the thick vines leading to the valley. We've been staying here for the past few months. We rarely venture out because it's too dangerous. Celest has been close to reaching us. She found where we're hidden weeks ago and has cast many spells to try to tear down the veil that protects us. But each time, she failed. We desperately need to find a way to be rid of her. We've been searching for a spell to cast her away, to no avail. Each time, we'd venture out as a group. But this time, I did it alone. This was something that I had to do on my own.

"Serenity!" Vincent calls as he jogs over to me, drawing me into his strong arms. His embrace feels like a protective shield, his familiar scent comforting me amidst the tension.

"Where the hell have you been?" Anger, mixed with relief, crosses his expression. His eyes search mine, a storm of emotions brewing within them.

"I found a way to be rid of Celest! A spell to banish her from Mirgora. It'll put a protective shield around our entire realm so she can never enter again," I say with excitement, my words tumbling out in a rush.

"And how did you find this spell? And why not tell us so we could at least go with you to protect you?" Vincent asks, irritation filling his tone. "Do you have any idea how dangerous and reckless that was? You could have been caught!"

"Sweetheart, don't be mad. I didn't tell you because if we had been caught, you could have been killed. I couldn't live with that. I was trying to protect you. All of you."

Vincent opens his mouth to respond, but before he can, Uncle steps in. "Enough. Both of you. Ren, how did you find this spell?" His authoritative tone demands an immediate answer.

"I went to the isle of Myria to speak with the elder Mirgorist. He said it was crucial we do this now. He didn't say why, but..." I trail off, my mind replaying the eerie journey to the mystical isle.

"The isle of Myria?" Uncle interrupts. "How did you find it? Sorcerers have been trying to find it for centuries!" His eyes widen in disbelief.

Arian chimes in now. "It was me. The same old man came to me in a dream. He told me Ren had to go to the isle of Myria immediately. He told me she could easily find it once she began her journey."

"She's right," I nod. "Somehow I did find it. Something led me right to it." I recall the strange pull that guided me through the dense forests and over treacherous terrain.

"Sir Edmond, Sir Vincent, I'm sorry for not telling you. The old man made me swear not to tell anyone about it." Arian's voice trembles with guilt.

Shock settles into Uncle's expression as he glances between Arian and me. "I don't believe it. Ren, do you have any idea what this means?"

"No, Uncle. What?" I ask skeptically, my heart pounding in anticipation.

"It has always been known that those who possess the ancient magic of Mirgora can find the island. The isle of Myria is the place where magic itself was born. There are only a handful of Mirgorists left, and it seems you're one of them." His words hang in the air, laden with significance.

I let out a nervous laugh. There is no way that's possible. "What exactly are you saying?" I ask, even though he already told me. Shock has made it impossible for me to grasp.

"What I'm saying is, you must be an elder of this land." His eyes bore into mine, willing me to understand the gravity of the situation.

I shake my head. "No, you must be wrong. There's no way I possess such powerful magic as you suggest." My voice is a mere whisper.

"Yes, you do," Arian chimes in. We all stare at her in silence, so she continues. "I've seen the power you possess in my dreams. You're so much stronger than Celest. You too, Sir Vincent," she says, looking between the both of us.

"Me?" Vincent asks skeptically, his brows furrowing in disbelief.

"Yes," Arian says matter-of-factly. "You both are much more powerful than you even know. In fact, Sir Vincent, you too are immortal."

"That can't be," he says, shaking his head.

"Yes, it can. And it is," she says to him.

Vincent looks over to me, and then back at Arian as he stands silently, taking it all in. Relief floods through me at her words. I have spent many sleepless nights knowing that I would live forever while Vincent grows old, eventually succumbing to his age. And I would be left alone, without him. The thought has haunted me for so long. But now, I never have to worry about that again. And I never have to worry about Celest chopping his head off again.

"What else have you seen?" I ask Arian, my voice trembling with a mix of hope and fear.

"It's just bits and pieces. Mostly quick flashes. I just see you using powerful magic. I don't see on who, though I'm guessing it's Celest."

Vincent and I remain silent. How is it possible that we're part of the elder Mirgorists of Myria and never knew it? I'm still not entirely convinced that that's what it is. Being an elder means being alive since the beginning of magic itself. As far as I recall, I've only been alive for twenty-eight years. Though it would explain the mysterious connection between Vincent and me.

"Ren, what is it this man told you to do?" Uncle asks, his tone urgent.

"He gave me this," I say, snapping myself from my thoughts. I pull a large coin out of my pocket and hand it to Uncle.

He examines it closely, flipping it over either side. "Amazing," he says in awe. "It bears the mark of the ancient religion. This is a very powerful weapon to wield."

"Do you think you can do it?" Arian asks, her eyes wide with anticipation.

I consider her question carefully. I never thought it possible for me to wield any type of magical weapon, much less one that bears the mark of the ancient religion. "The man said it had to be at to-night's full moon, as the clock strikes one. He said we'd know exactly what to do when the time came."

"We?" Vincent asks, his voice laced with concern. I nod as I walk over to him. "You're a crucial part of this, Vincent. The Mirgor said only with you will the spell be complete. Our powers combined are needed."

He wraps his arms around me, hugging me tight. "I have no idea what that means. But I'm with you, always." His lips graze against mine before kissing me softly, sending chills to my core.

"I have no idea what it means either," I say. And that thought alone is enough to terrify me. So much could go wrong, especially since this is my first time casting such a powerful spell.

"There's something else I need to tell you all, in case this spell doesn't work," Arian says, her voice tinged with urgency.

"What is it?" I ask, my heart pounding in my chest.

She purses her lips together, unsure of how to deliver the news. "I had another vision right before you returned. Celest, she has a weapon to kill you both. It's some sort of amulet. I was told it's the only one known to kill immortal beings."

The blood in my veins turns to ice. I was naïve to think that just because we're immortal, we must be invincible. Of course, there is a weapon to kill us. There was a way to destroy just about anything if you tried hard enough. And now, I have to worry about Celest getting to Vincent once more.

"Who told you, Arian?" Vincent asks, his voice tight with tension.

"The same man I always see in my visions. He said if for some reason the spell doesn't hold, we'd need to go in search of a weapon to destroy her before she does you."

"Why not just steal the one she has and kill her with it?" I ask, beginning to feel weak with worry as I touch my hand to my forehead.

"Because it won't work on her. I don't know how or why. All I know is what my visions tell me."

"It's the stake of Albitar," Uncle says, his voice grave.

"The stake of what?" I ask, my mind reeling.

"It's a stake to kill immortals. It's filled with dark magic that only a dark sorceress like Celest can wield. Its wood comes from the city of Albitar, known only for its practice of the dark arts."

Vincent's jaw clenches. "Well then, we better hope the spell works." His eyes meet mine, a silent vow passing between us. We have to make this work. For our future. For everything we hold dear.

Chapter 18

As I sit by the fire, I become mesmerized by the dance of its flames. They flicker and sway so effortlessly, almost as if they're floating in a rhythmic dance. Their shadows bounce just as happily on the ground at my feet, casting fleeting images that play with my imagination. Tiny sparks shoot out, reaching for the sky, only to fade away into the blackness above, mirroring the fleeting thoughts that race through my mind.

I shiver, feeling the cool air wrap itself around me with force, almost like a tangible presence. There's a certain heaviness to it tonight, an ominous weight that seems to press down on everything, as though the earth is preparing for what's to come. The weight of the coin in my pocket grabs my attention, and I take it out, flipping it between my fingers. It appears to be made of solid gold. An ancient scripture is carved around its rim in a language I've never seen before. One side bears a large, majestic tree, and the other a mysterious symbol. A strange sensation pulses from the coin and up into my arm. It's almost like the pulsating between Vincent and me, but not quite as strong. It feels strangely familiar, as if it belongs to me, though I've never seen a coin like it in my life.

"Are you nervous?" Vincent asks as he sits down next to me, his presence instantly calming yet electrifying.

I rest my head on his shoulder, nuzzling against his neck. The warmth of his skin contrasts with the coolness of the night, creating a perfect balance. "A little," I admit, my voice barely above a whisper.

"I know we can do this. There isn't anything we can't do as long as we're together," he says, his confidence unwavering.

"I know we can. I can feel it," I say with a smile, the weight of the coin seeming to grow lighter in my hand.

I pause for a moment, recalling my time spent with the elder Mirgor. "He bowed to me when I approached him," I finally say, the memory vivid in my mind.

"Who did?" Vincent asks, turning his head to look at me, his eyes filled with curiosity.

"The Mirgor. It was as though he worshipped me. And then he said he had been waiting for this moment for a long time. What does that mean, do you think? How have I been unaware of my abilities my entire life? The Mirgor seemed to know me. But how is that possible? I've never seen him before, and I knew nothing of him until today."

Vincent thought for a moment, a devilish grin playing at the corner of his mouth. "Maybe you're a goddess," he teases. "You look like one, anyway."

"Very funny," I say as I playfully nudge his shoulder, though the thought lingers in my mind.

Vincent glances down at the coin, curiosity settling into his expression. "Let me see this for a second," he says as he takes the coin from me. He flips it over, looking confused, his brow furrowing in concentration.

"What's the matter?" I ask.

"Nothing. It's just..." He stops as he fishes around in his pocket. He pulls out a pendant necklace, inspecting it along with the coin. "I found this today when I went to the village looking for you. A man had it in his shop. I was so drawn to it, I couldn't walk away, and I knew it was meant for you," he says as he hands the necklace to me.

As soon as it falls into my palm, I feel the same vibrating current as the coin, and I gasp at its beauty. The pendant is circular with a large tree forged in the center, its branches plush and full. The leaves are made of tiny diamonds that sparkle eagerly under the moonlight.

"Oh, Vincent," I breathe. "It's so beautiful!"

"Look at the back," he says in a low voice, his eyes reflecting the soft glow of the fire.

I turn it over and see an engraving:

"I love you with all my heart and soul -V.A."

I let out a breath, choking back happy tears as I look up at him. "Vincent...I will cherish this always," I say, my voice thick with emotion, as I hug his neck.

"It's my promise to you, Serenity. That we will always be together. And no matter what gets in our way, we'll overcome it," he says against my ear, his breath warm and reassuring. He takes the necklace from me briefly before placing gently hands around the back of my neck, clasping it in place. I instinctively reach up to touch it, the warm current of the necklace humming on my chest and penetrating my heart with eternal bliss.

I kiss him deeply, our lips moving in rhythm with one another. I place my hand on his chest, feeling the steady beating of his heart against my palm. The warmth of his body envelops me, the buzzing of his touch coursing wildly through my veins. And as if I didn't already know, it's in this moment that I realize there's so much more to our love than simply feelings. I can feel it soaring through my heart like a volcanic eruption. The power. The magic. The destiny that brought us together. And I know together, we can achieve great things.

Uncle clears his throat, and I jolt back, embarrassed that he caught us in an intimate moment. The gravity of the situation quickly returns, grounding me back to the reality of our mission.

"It's almost time," Arian says as she and Uncle walk up to us, her eyes wide with anticipation.

I let out a nervous sigh. "Here goes nothing, I guess," I say, my voice shaking slightly.

Vincent stands, pulling me up with him. Together, we make our way over to the small fire, Uncle and Arian close behind. The fire dances in rhythm with the cool breeze, appearing very much alive. There's a sudden shift in the atmosphere, sending shivers down my spine. It feels as though the air itself is charged with energy, the very essence of magic swirling around us.

"What now?" Arian asks, her voice trembling with a mix of excitement and fear.

I was about to say I didn't know what to do as I prepared myself for automatic failure, but something shifted inside of me in that moment.

Knowledge of the spell comes crashing through me like a bolt of lightning, its energy making me feel more alive than I ever have before. I let out a gasp, and Vincent clasps both of his hands in mine. We look at each other now, fully aware of what needs to be done.

"Uncle, Arian, stand on either side of us, please. It's beginning."

They quickly position themselves next to Vincent and me, waiting in anticipation. Vincent pulls out the coin, dropping it between us. It begins to glow brightly, reminding me of the time when we first kissed. The way our skin lit up, sending a surge of energy through us and creating a power I never knew could exist. This feels the same. The same color, the same feel. The coin is very much alive as we begin to chant.

"We reach out to our ancestors, the Mirgorists of the past, present, and future, to help us in our darkest hour. Give us the strength and the power to rid ourselves of the evil that seeks to destroy us. We

ask you this now, to banish Celest, Queen of Duix, from Mirgora forever."

A bolt of lightning shoots from the coin, splitting the sky with a vengeance. Thunder crashes loudly, shaking the ground beneath my feet. A soft, white glow surrounds each of us, and I clasp Vincent's hand tighter in anticipation. This is it. We will finally be free of Celest.

The ground shakes viciously as the leaves and branches covering the valley begin to open. The black sky whirls around us so ferociously, the entire veil around the valley collapses, leaving us completely exposed. I look up at Vincent, fear taking over. This is not part of the spell. I can feel the spell we just cast, and this was not it. This is something different entirely.

"What's happening?" Arian screeches through the howling wind.

"I don't know!" I yell back, panic rising in my chest.

The ground shakes with such force now that I'm having a hard time standing. I clasp onto Vincent to hold my balance while he puts his arm tightly around me. The wind is whipping through us at such speeds that it forces its way into my nostrils, and I gasp for air, feeling as though I'm suffocating. Arian falls to her knees, looking up at the black sky with her arms outstretched, letting out a blood-curdling scream. I quickly stumble over to her, staring down at her in horror.

"Arian! What's wrong?"

The ground shakes steadily, making me lose my balance. I quickly grasp her shoulder to hold myself up, and she grabs my wrist with such force that I'm afraid it may break. She looks up at me, her eyes cold and dark. My heart beats wildly in my chest as I look at my friend, barely recognizable now.

"I'm coming for you, my darling," she says in a cold tone that makes me grow weak. "You have nowhere left to hide. I hope you've enjoyed these months with your precious lover, for they were your last!" The rain begins to pour in sheets, and a wicked laugh escapes Arian's lips as her head tilts up to the sky.

I stumble back, my heart feeling like it will pound right out of my chest. Celest. She was the one who took down the veil; that's why it felt different from the spell we cast. Her dark magic crept through like a slithering snake sizing up its prey.

Arian's eyes clear, fear gripping her expression.

"Serenity, she's coming! Right now!" Arian cries, her voice filled with terror.

"You and Vincent have to leave! Now!" Uncle yells over the howling wind and downpour.

"What about you?" I ask frantically as I grip his arms.

"I'll hold her off. You have to go now!" he says, kissing my forehead. "I love you so much, Ren. Don't ever forget that. And I promise when I see you again, I'll tell you everything I know."

"Everything you know?" I ask, desperate for answers.

"There's no time to explain now," he says urgently. He looks over to Vincent. "Take her as far away from here as possible. I'll look after Arian."

Vincent quickly grabs my hand, leading us into the dark night. I look back at Uncle and Arian one more time. Uncle watches as we walk away, his eyes full of sadness and determination as he nods, silently urging me to keep going. Arian is still kneeling on the ground, the harsh rain soaking her to the bone as she clings to Uncle's hand. I don't know when, or if, I'll ever see them again, and the thought crushes my heart.

As we plunge into the darkness, the gaping presence of the forest swallows us whole. The rain beats down relentlessly, the wind howling through the trees, making the path ahead treacherous. The forest, usually a place of solace, now feels like a labyrinth of shadows and dangers.

Chapter 19

The rain is coming down in sheets, the drops pounding viciously into the sand. Lightning streaks across the sky, reminding me of roots forcing their way beneath the soil, and the thunder booms loud enough to vibrate in my chest. In the distance is a cave, carved into a giant cliffside. To my left, the sea churns angrily, the waves crashing and moaning in rhythm with the storm.

My pace begins to slow, no matter how hard I try to keep running. The icy water splashes up around my ankles, making my legs feel numb and heavy. Each step feels like I'm trudging through thick mud, my body resisting the urge to collapse.

"Ren, we have to keep moving! She's coming!" Vincent yells over the rain. His words are frantic, but his eyes show something entirely different. They're gentle, loving, filled with an unspoken promise.

I want nothing more than to drop to my knees and curl up in a ball until this all goes away. Exhaustion has settled in, my lungs burning with each excruciating step I take. We've been on the run for hours, over rough mountain terrain. The forest seemed never-ending as branches smacked across my face, blood blinding me as it trickled into my eyes. Through thick brush that scratched my shins, the saltwater splashing into the scratches made it that much worse.

"I don't think I can!" I cry. And it was true. I've never felt so defeated in my life.

"Yes, you can, love. You have to!" Vincent says as he clasps my hand tighter, practically dragging me across the sand to the cliffside. The rain mixes with our sweat, making our grip slippery, but he never lets go.

"We'll wait it out in here. We can't keep going with this storm," he says as he looks the cave over. The cave is small, much smaller than I expected against the massive cliff, its presence hiding so well, we almost missed it. The walls are black, small crystals scattered against the dark contrast. They shimmered happily, though there was no light to reflect them. It's as though the cave is alive, protecting us from the dangers that lurked so nearby. The air inside is cool and damp, carrying the faint smell of earth and salt.

"She can't do this to us," I say, anger burning deep into my heart as if to consume me. We finally found a way to rid her of this realm forever, only to have it ripped away from us. Our lives are once again in danger, and the looming question of "why" nags at my mind. Why is she so hell-bent on keeping us apart, to the point she's willing to kill us? I've always known she hates me, but to go to such

extremes to see me dead is a completely different level of hate. It's loathing. It's... fear.

Vincent gently cups my face, his gaze so deep, it pierces into my soul in warm, soothing waves. "We will never be apart. We are so much stronger than she is," he says in a soft tone.

Though I knew that to be mostly true, I don't know how we're stronger. How do we go about destroying the indestructible?

"She has a weapon, Vincent. She will kill us!" Hysteria trickles to the surface, and I quickly force it back.

"Trust me," he says in a low voice. "We will defeat her. I can feel it, just as I can feel you now." He touches his hand to my chest, feeling my beating heart. I place my hand on his as I close my eyes, taking in his touch for as long as I can. The warmth of his palm is a stark contrast to the cold rain that soaks us.

"How?" I finally ask. "She's immortal."

"So are we," he points out.

"But she has the stone of Albitar! We have nothing!"

"I know. But we'll find a way to kill her. It's out there somewhere." His eyes turn dark as he continues. "I will never stop looking. I'll go to the ends of the world, and in every corner. And if that doesn't work, I'll go beyond. I'll search every realm until we find what we're looking for. Because I refuse to lose you. I love you more than anything." His eyes flicker

in the flash of the lightning, and the passion in his voice makes my knees weaken.

My heart bursts with love as he holds me in his solid arms. I tilt my head up, our lips grazing softly against one another. He kisses me now with such intense passion, I fear I may faint. The electricity between us is palpable, a force of nature in its own right.

I back away slightly, hearing a loud crack near the sea. It sounded tremendously different than thunder, so I know it isn't that. It had more of a scream to it than a rumble, a piercing cry that seemed to come from the depths of the ocean itself.

"What was that?" I ask. I touch my forehead, still feeling very much dizzy from our kiss.

"I didn't hear anything," he says as he scans the area, his eyes narrowing in concentration.

The dizziness increases as my soul begins to feel like it's fading away. This isn't anything I've ever felt kissing Vincent before. This is something more...

"Vincent," I screech as I hold onto my head. "Vincent, something is wrong!"

"Ren, what is it? What's wrong?" he asks, panic filling his voice as he holds me steady.

"I don't know. It's... it's..."

The world around me spins out of control, the pressure in my head growing at an extreme rate. I begin to fall backward, unable to stand any longer. Vincent quickly reaches for me, attempting to stop the fall, but catches my necklace instead as it rips from my neck.

"Serenity!" I can hear Vincent cry in the distance. But I could form no words as I fall into a dark abyss, everything around me becoming all too silent. I can feel my soul lift from my body, leaving me an empty vessel as despair shudders its way through. My existence has been torn away before it could ever truly begin.

Chapter 20

I let out a chilling scream as I bolt upright in bed, grabbing at my chest, desperate to coax the air back into my lungs. The empty feeling of having no soul, no matter how brief, has left an angry scar on my heart.

"Serenity!" Vincent is sitting on the bed with me, his eyes feral as fear takes hold. He reaches out, his hands trembling slightly, as if he's afraid I might disappear again.

It takes some time to comprehend, but I feel different somehow, almost like I'm a completely different person. I feel bolder, stronger. The power that sweeps through me feels like I'm finally waking up for the first time in years. I glance around the room, everything appearing sharper, more vivid, as if my senses have been heightened.

A million memories come flooding into my mind as I recall every moment I've ever spent with Vincent. Every detail of my childhood and life before him comes to me just as fast. The life that was once stolen from me is back. I have no doubts about who I am anymore. I know without a doubt, I am Serenity, princess of Duix.

Though I'll be relinquishing that title just as soon as I get my hands on Celest.

I look at Vincent now, really look at him through eyes that have been closed to me for so long. Part of me hasn't been with him for twenty-eight years, and I give a brief thanks to the ancient Mirgors above that I at least have the other memory of only two years away from him. It made the pain a little more manageable.

Seeing him now brings a happiness to me that makes my heart burst with pride. I finally have my life back. I finally have him back.

"Oh, my Gods. Vincent," I cry as I hug him, my chest pressed firmly against his. "I have missed you so much."

He pulls away slightly, looking at me quizzically. "Ren?" he asks, excitement filling his tone.

I nod happily as tears spill from my eyes. "It's me, sweetheart. I found my way back to you," I say in a whisper, my voice trembling with emotion.

He lets out a relieved sigh as tears threaten the edge of his eyelids. "Thank Gods," he says as he pulls me in, wrapping his arms tightly around me. "I thought I was losing you again, like I did that night in the cave."

"You are never going to lose me again," I promise him, my lips grazing softly against his cheek.

He pulls back slightly to peer into my eyes, his gaze soft and full of adoration. He notices the shimmer of my necklace on my chest as the sunlight beams through the window, making it sparkle with life.

He lets out a happy sigh. “You found it,” he says as he traces it with his fingertip.

I nod my head, a tear slipping down my cheek. “I had a tree of my own in the other world. It looked exactly like this necklace. I found it after the light came to me the first time. It’s how I knew without a doubt you were real.”

“A key part of the spell to get you back to our world was using something that belonged to you. Your uncle had many things, but I knew this would be the one thing that would help you find your way back to us. To me,” he says in a soft tone.

“It worked,” I say. “I’ve had it on since the day I found it. It has brought me so much peace when I felt like everything about my life was falling apart.”

He smiles softly as he reaches up to brush the hair out of my eyes, his fingertips lightly tracing my ear.

Feeling his touch against me, now that I remember who I am, sends a spark through my core. It's unlike anything I've ever felt before, as my body trembles with excitement. I love this man with every ounce of my soul and every fiber of my being. I place my hand on his chest, feeling the steady beating of his heart. I close my eyes, taking in the feeling of having him back, feeling his touch again.

Despite the overwhelming feeling of happiness and love filling my heart, I get a sense of dread.

Now that I have my powers back, I can feel Celest is back in this realm with us.

"We need to find Uncle," I say. A sudden unease wraps itself around me as I shudder. Celest knows that I've been trying to find my way back, and now that I'm here, I fear she may be able to sense it just as I sense her. It won't be long before she becomes aware of my presence back in this realm. And when she does, she'll be coming for me.

Vincent nods, sensing my fear. "I know right where he'll be," he says.

We ride for most of the day, heading north, a direction I've never ventured off to before. Celest had never let me get too far from the surrounding villages of Duix. But now, as the bark on the trees turns to a vibrant color of gold and the forest floor shines brightly even against the darkening sky, I know we're no longer in Celest's kingdom. I can feel the magic vibrating excitedly through my veins the farther we venture into this unknown territory, and I smile at its sensation. It's the same as when Vincent and I touch.

"What is this place?" I ask, turning my head from side to side, taking in my unnatural surroundings. The trees seem to hum with energy, their leaves rustling in a way that feels almost like a whispered welcome.

"It's the kingdom of Myria," Vincent says.

"The…" I stop myself as a nervous excitement washes through me. I couldn't remember before why this place felt so familiar, but now it's crystal clear. It was the same feeling, the same look as when I went to the Isle of Myria to find the artifact to banish Celest from this realm.

"There's a whole Kingdom of Myrgorists?" I ask in awe, my eyes widening as I take in the beauty around me. The air feels charged with ancient magic, making the hairs on my arms stand on end.

Vincent's expression saddens, but he quickly regains his composure. "There really aren't too many left. There are only a few High Priests and Priestesses left."

"How have I never known of this place before?" I ask.

"Celest, for one. She had it hidden it from you, so you'd never become aware."

My heart begins to pound as anger heats my cheeks. Why would she ever keep this place from me? What possible reason could she have? It's not like I know any of the ancient Mirgorists here.

"Why would she do that?" I ask through gritted teeth as anger begins to bubble up once more. I'm having a hard time deciphering why, but I feel immensely betrayed.

"You'll learn everything soon. We're almost there," Vincent says, nodding ahead.

I follow his gaze, and my breath catches in my throat. The sight I'm seeing is unlike anything I've ever seen before. Just ahead of us lies a large city. All the homes on the outer lying villages appear to be that of any other home. Beyond the villages, built into a mountain, is a castle beaming proudly. Its golden exterior shines brightly against the blackness of the night, just as the forest floor did.

Once we approach the gate leading into the villages, the door opens approvingly as if it were expecting us. As the gate exposes its interior to us, the wave of magic inside hits me with force. It's the same buzzing feeling I've felt so many times before, but a little different from what I feel with Vincent. This feeling reminds me more of the night we touched the coin I found at the Isle of Myria to banish Celest…

"Brace yourself," Vincent says, looking straight ahead. His expression is filled with worry, as if he's remembering something unpleasant about this place.

My stomach turns to knots as Juniper moves forward and through the gates. I can feel the ground beneath her hooves vibrating with the same energy coursing through me.

When we finally reach the lower part of the castle grounds, the magic coursing through me becomes almost too much to bear. The power crashes through my veins like ice as I wince over my horse in pain.

"Vincent, there's something wrong," I say through gritted teeth.

"Yes, they'll explain everything inside," Vincent says. His voice sounds different than normal, so I glance over at him. He too appears to be in as much anguish as I'm feeling. My heart stops as I look him over. The veins in his neck begin to protrude as if something has become alive inside of him. As I look closer, I notice that his veins are glowing a yellow-gold color. My mind instantly returns to the night we shared our first kiss in the stables back at Duix. When we touched our lips together for the first time, our bodies radiated the same soft glow as what I'm seeing now.

Curious, I glance down at my hands. To my surprise, the veins in my wrists and hands are glowing the same color as Vincent's. I'm slowly beginning to realize that all of this—me and Vincent, this place, Celest—it's all connected in some way. There is something much greater happening here than I can even begin to comprehend. But before I can think too much more about it, I'm gently pulled off Juniper and escorted into the towering castle, Vincent close behind.

The pain and the power coursing through me intensify as we walk into the castle. So much so that I can't focus on who we are approaching. Voices are muffled, and my vision blurs to the point that I can't see even a couple of inches ahead of me. I feel a gentle hand grip my shoulder. "Let's get you fixed up."

The voice, muffled and indistinct, could be male or female. I'm not sure if anyone is really talking or if it's just my imagination. But finally, just when I'm beginning to think I've completely lost my mind, the fog in my head begins to clear, and so does my vision. The muffled voices turn crisp and clear as I snap my head up to look at them.

The first person I notice is Uncle Edmond, standing just as tall and proud as the last day I saw him, almost three decades ago. But then I realize, it has only been two years here.

"Uncle," I say as I rush over to him. He embraces me in a tight hug, and I close my eyes, taking in the familiar feeling of the man who raised me. I hadn't realized until this moment how much I truly missed him.

"Ren. Oh, thank the gods," he says, his voice breaking as emotion takes over. "I was beginning to think we lost you for good."

"She's a strong young woman. I knew she could do it," a man says.

I glance over at him, memories of the day at the Isle of Myria rushing back to me.

"You," I say.

"Yes, my lady. My name is Redrich. It is a pleasure to see you again."

I nod to him as I look around the room. The interior is just as magnificent as the exterior. The walls are solid gold, sprawling up to the bright and glistening ceiling. The floors are marbled with gold and silver, swirling around and meshing together perfectly. In the center of the room is a large, winding staircase, its steps and rails matching the rest.

"What is this place?" I ask in awe.

Vincent puts a gentle hand on my shoulder and smiles at me warmly. My knees become weak with hunger for him the closer he gets. I push that feeling aside the best I can as I try to keep my focus. Thoughts of having Vincent in my bed distract me from the real reason we are here, whatever that may be.

"There is much to tell you," Redrich says. "Please, let's go to the sitting room where we'll be more comfortable."

We quickly make our way into the next room over, looking very much like every other part of the castle. There's a fireplace on the far end of the room, wood crackling peacefully against the dancing flames. A couch and two chairs sit directly in front of it, and to the right side of the fire, is an old wooden desk carved in intricate detail along the legs. As I examine it closer, I notice the design is familiar. On the front side of the desk is a large tree, its branches stemming out around the legs of the desk. I look up to see Redrich smiling at me fondly.

"That's a look of familiarity, and rightfully so," he says.

I furrow my brow as I look at him inquisitively. Somehow, all of this is connected, and apparently, so is this tree. I've seen it many times. The first time I remember seeing it was on the coin Redrich gave me for the banishing spell. And at the same time as I was retrieving the coin, Vincent found a necklace with the same tree. And of course, the tree in the field in the other realm where the door to this realm first appeared to me. But what it all means is a mystery beyond my wildest imaginations.

"Sit," he says as he ushers us to the sitting area. "I know you're eager to learn who you are, or rather, what you are."

Chapter 21

We sit in silence for what seems to be an eternity as the maids silently busy themselves with retrieving tea for each of us. Redrich's demeanor is relaxed as he plops some sugar into his tea and swirls it around with his finger. He takes a sip, pleased by its sweet taste, a small smile playing on his lips. Next, he pulls a pipe from his pocket, and a maid quickly ushers over with matches to light it for him. He puffs slowly a few times, taking in the strong scent of the tobacco before finally settling back into his chair.

I watch him closely, gripping the teacup with force. I nervously scratch away at its edges, fearing I'll eventually break right through, making my nails bleed in the process.

"So, I suppose you're wondering why you're here," Redrich begins.

"The thought has crossed my mind a time or two," I say carefully.

He lets out a booming laugh as he leans forward in the chair. "Still just as charismatic as you've always been, my dear. Time has not changed that in the least."

I look at him, confused. "I know it's been nearly three decades for, well, part of me. But hasn't it only been two years for you?" I ask. As far as I recall, I never did or said anything the one time I did meet him to make him laugh, since I was there on a serious matter.

"Three decades passed for you?" Uncle asks in awe.

"Yes," I say with a nod. "Kind of, anyway. That part of me remembers three decades. But once my memories came back to me, this part of me feels like it's only been two years." None of it made sense, and I couldn't even make sense of it myself, but I don't bother to comment further.

"Astonishing," Redrich says. "But my dear, I have known you for much, much longer than that. And I have known Vincent for just as long."

I look over to Vincent, who is now softly gripping my hand, giving me a reassuring smile. His touch calms me tremendously. I know that Vincent would never put me in any kind of danger, and I know that he already knows what I'm about to be told. He said I would know everything soon, meaning he must already know. And if it were bad, he wouldn't have brought me here to begin with. Uncle Edmond wouldn't be here either.

"How long is 'much longer'?" I ask as I look back at Redrich.

He clasps his hands together, tapping his two pointer fingers. "About eight hundred years."

I choke down the tea as I look at him in disbelief. Did he just say...eight hundred years? There's no way that can be possible. Sure, I lost my memories of this life when I was in the other realm, but I regained them as soon as I was back here. I remember everything about this life. My childhood, my wretched mother, the loss of my father at such a young age, and Uncle Edmond stepping in and taking care of me as if I were his own. There is no way all of that happened over the course of so many centuries.

"That doesn't make any sense," I say in shock. Vincent grips my hand tighter as he senses my growing anxiety.

"I know it's hard to understand, Serenity. But you have lived through many lifetimes, losing you being equally as devastating each time."

"Losing me? You're saying I've...died before?"

Redrich nods. "Many times. Seven, to be precise."

I let out a nervous laugh as my heart quickens. All of this must be some sort of joke.

"How is that even possible?" I ask, not entirely believing what I've been told.

"You and Vincent are some of the first Mirgorists to walk this realm. In fact, in your first life, you helped build this city."

I stare at him in silence for a long moment as he waits patiently for me to answer.

"You're saying I am an ancient Mirgorist who helped build this city to begin with?" I ask as I stand. I look back at him, shaking my head. "I'm sorry, but I just don't believe it."

Redrich stands and walks over to me. "May I show you something?" he asks, his expression soft and calm, no trace of irritation with me not entirely believing his wild story.

When I only stare at him in disbelief, Vincent quickly stands with me, cupping my face in his hands as he scans his soft eyes over mine. “Ren, I know this is a lot to take in. But please listen to what he has to say. There is so much about ourselves, about us, that we’ve always wanted to know. Redrich has those answers.”

Vincent’s touch soothes my anxiety considerably as I concentrate on the vibrating sensation his skin creates against mine. His hands. Those incredibly warm hands against my skin make my heart go wild with need. A primal need for him that I can’t even begin to describe. I feel the heat rising in my cheeks as I secretly fantasize about his hands on me in other places. Places a little lower than where they are now.

A devilish grin plays on the corner of his lips as if he’s reading my thoughts. I smile back, my eyes searing into him just as devilishly as that knee-weakening grin of his.

Redrich interrupts our moment with a clearing of his throat. As painful as it is, I pry my eyes away from Vincent to look over at him.

“May I?” Redrich asks as he comes closer to me.

"Certainly," I finally say.

He gently cups my face in his hands and closes his eyes. The warmth of his skin courses through me like fire, but it's surprisingly calming. I close my eyes with him as my soul begins to feel like it's drifting from my body. Images flash rapidly through my mind, and I have a hard time keeping up with it all. It feels oddly familiar, as if I've seen all of this before. Some part of me feels a sense of sentiment as flashes of the City of Myria being built cross my mind. There, in the midst of it all, are Vincent and I, using our power to build the city and the very castle we're standing in. We're happy, wrapped in each other's arms, laughing like there's nothing in the world to worry about. Uncle Edmond is there with us. An older man I can't quite place is there too; his warm embrace feels so much like home…like love. Not the same kind of love as Vincent, of course. This is something else. This is a different kind of bond entirely.

Finally, the last images come flooding in, and the feeling of peace quickly turns to terror. I see myself in a long, white dress. It fits tightly at my bodice, showing every curve all the way down to my waist. From there, the dress flows like a gentle breeze down to my feet. Vincent is dressed just as magnificently. Though his white shirt flows loosely around his torso, you can easily see his muscles bulging beneath it. One button is undone, showing just a little bit of the hair on his chest. As we walk toward each other, I then see Vincent and I being ripped away from one another, and I watch as Celest plunges a giant wooden stake through his heart. The life quickly fades from his eyes as blood trickles from his mouth. He's staring at me as he takes his final breath, and I let out a scream loud enough to shake the ground below me. Celest seems completely unfazed and unharmed by my outburst of magic because, in the blink of an eye, she is standing directly in front of me, her expression filled with contentment as she takes the stake, still soaked in Vincent's blood, to my heart next. I feel pain in my chest like I've never felt before as the world around me goes dark. I know it was in that moment that Vincent and I died side by side.

Redrich lets go of me, and the flashing images finally stop as I drop to my knees. Gut-wrenching screams escape my lips as I sob uncontrollably. It takes me a moment to realize I'm no longer in the nightmare of our deaths, and it isn't until Vincent crouches down beside me and wraps his arms tightly around me that I snap out of it. I don't speak for a long time as I try to fight for air and the feeling of seeing Vincent's death from my heart. I focus on the feeling of his lips against my cheek as he whispers in my ear. "Everything is alright now. I'm right here, love. I'll never let anything like that happen to us again." His reassuring words course through me like a cool drink of water on a scorching summer day, and I finally relax into him.

"That was our first life together," I say matter-of-factly. I don't question it, for I know it to be true. I could feel every little thing I felt from that life eight hundred years ago, as if I had just lived it.

"Yes," Redirch says as Vincent helps me to my feet. We sit back down in our seats as my shaking legs begin to recover.

"Did we die like that every time?" I ask.

"No. In fact, that was the only other time you and Vincent knew each other. Celest would always have you both killed at a young age, sometimes even as infants, so you could never meet again."

"Why?" I ask through gritted teeth as the anger begins to bubble up inside of me. "Why does she want us apart so bad?"

"Because you two have the weapon to kill her. In fact, you are the only ones who can kill her."

My head snaps up as my gaze pierces into his. "What do you mean we have the weapon? What is the weapon?"

Redrich smiles fondly now as he looks between Vincent and me. "You two are the weapon. Tell me, have you felt the hunger burning inside of you? The hunger to...have him?" he asks.

My face burns hot with embarrassment as I remember our night together in the tent. How close we were to making love that night, and all the ways we explored each other's bodies. My heart begins to race as I grip Vincent's hand tighter. I know he's remembering that night too, for his pulse is quick against mine. And then I remember the demanding voice telling us to stop. In fact, I can now place whose voice that was.

"It was you that night telling us to stop," I say. He nods his head slowly. "But why?" I ask.

"Because there are very strict steps to follow if this is to work. For you to become the weapon to destroy Celest, you first need to unite in matrimony. After the ancient Mirgorian ceremony takes place, you must unite yourselves as one by sharing the marriage bed. If you were to have shared your bodies with one another the night that I stopped you, matrimony would have been void, and the uniting of souls would never take place."

"Uniting of souls?" is all I can think to ask.

"Indeed," Redrich nods. "Your souls have been meant for each other since the very beginning of time. Even in death, you have always been but one soul. It is now in life that you must unite those souls together once again. Once that takes place, the powerful force between you will be stronger than anything known to the whole of the universe."

I let out a breath as I let it all sink in. Everything Redrich has said explains so much. It explains why Celest looked so terrified when Vincent first came to Duix and why she forbade me from seeing him. And it explains the burning passion Vincent and I have for one another. It's why we could never stay apart even if we tried. Our souls have been united since the beginning of creation. And somehow, even though our conscious minds were unaware, our souls knew.

I look over to Uncle Edmond now, who is staring at me intently. "You knew this whole time?" I ask. I saw him in the visions I had. He had been there since the beginning with me. He had to have known.

"No, darling. I didn't know. Like you, Celest would kill me too, and my memories would be erased. Do you remember when I left after Celest caught us talking about Vincent in my chambers? I said I was going for more recruits. I wasn't. I was looking for answers, and I finally found them. You see, I always knew there was something off about my life. I have no memories of my childhood whatsoever. Celest always told me that I had an accident causing me to lose all memories of my life up until adulthood. Come to find out, I somehow would come back every time you were born again. But I always came back as an adult, unlike you. And then, when Vincent came to Duix, I knew without a doubt there was something more happening. I had to find those answers. For both of us."

My head spins as I try to take in everything I've learned today. Never would I have thought any of this was possible. Especially that I'm not only a Mirgorist, but one of the first. That I have lived this life for centuries and it's all for a purpose.

"Why didn't Celest kill us as children this time around?" I ask.

"Your father," Uncle Edmond smiles.

"My…my father?"

Uncle nods. "He searched for centuries trying to find a way to stop Celest from harming either of you. Finally, during this century, he found a protection spell. It would stop Celest from harming you both just long enough to find one another again. Unfortunately, the spell doesn't last forever. That's why it's imperative we kill her once and for all."

“With that being said, there is one more thing you should know,” Redrich says, his tone serious. The concerning expression on his face sends my anxiety into overdrive.

“Go on,” I press.

“This is your last lifetime. Your last chance at uniting your souls. It has been known since the beginning that the time frame for this to take place was eight hundred years,” he says softly.

My heart pounds fiercely in my chest as Vincent grabs my hand, his anxiety soaring to immeasurable heights along with mine. I get a sense he knew nothing of this part with the way his pulse is crashing into mine.

“This year is the eight hundredth year,” uncle says.

“That seems ridiculous,” Vincent says now, his tone sharp with a mixture of fear.

Redrich nods. “Your souls have grown increasingly impatient over the years. They will be together one way or another. That’s why, Serenity, your father worked so hard in this lifetime to make sure you stayed alive, and together.”

I shake my head as panic sets in. If we don’t complete the ceremony in this lifetime, Vincent and I will never have a chance to truly be together. The thought sends the bile in my stomach into overdrive as it threatens to spill over on to the floor. I instinctively put a hand to my mouth and Vincent wraps his arms around me, attempting to sooth my ever-growing nerves. I cling to him tightly, the thought of us both losing our lives before we had a chance to even begin was too much to even consider.

"We aren't going to let that happen," uncle says now, in a soft voice, sadness filling his tone. "I'll never let anything happen to either of you."

A tear runs down my cheek. The anger of everything Celest has ever done throughout eight-hundred years to keep us a part has risen from a simmer to a raging boil within my blood. Why is she so threatened by us? Why couldn't she have just let us be, and then she wouldn't have to worry about us being powerful enough to kill her? If she could have just been the mother to me I deserved, we wouldn't be here today.

But that doesn't matter anymore. The fact of the matter is, this is happening, and we are here today. And I'm damn well going to finish it. I will not let her destroy us.

"You must be going now," Redrich says. "The spell I put on you to ward off the pain won't last much longer. We will talk again soon."

I had forgotten about the feeling of ice in my veins when we first arrived at the castle. But now, as he reminded me, I can feel the spell beginning to slowly fade away. A small ache, a mild chill, begins to fill me once more, and I shiver.

"Why does that happen?" I ask.

"It is the power within you waiting to resurface. It is your souls trying to pull together to be united once again. It is becoming more persistent, more demanding each time your mission has failed. This time, your souls will try at all costs to be together…even if that means ripping from your bodies to do so. That pain will cease completely once the unity is complete."

I don't question him any further. I'm far too exhausted to retain any more knowledge of my existence right now. All I care to do now is to be alone with Vincent and my thoughts.

Chapter 22

It is late when we leave the castle, but staying any longer wasn't an option for Vincent and me. The ice coursing through our veins subsides the farther we go, and once we stride through the gates and back into the forest, it disappears completely. All that is left is the faint hum of residual magic from the castle. But it was a feeling I'd grown to know and find comfort in over the years. Even as a human in the other realm, I could still feel the tingling of magic in my hands every time I dreamt of this life and Vincent. This has always been part of me, a crucial part of who I am.

"We're here," Vincent says, snapping me from my thoughts.

I glance around, trying to see where exactly we were. We hadn't been traveling for long, only a half hour or so, so I knew we hadn't made it back to Duix. The shimmering of the forest floor and the luminescent glow of the bark on the trees told me we were still in Myria. But nowhere did I see any kind of shelter. So, where exactly are we?

"Where is here?" I ask.

"Your home," Vincent says as he helps me dismount Juniper.

I look around again, scanning the area for any indication of a home or even a shack, but there is nothing but trees as far as I can see. However, the more I concentrate on the area, a strange sense of familiarity hits me.

I have been here before.

"This is where I lived in my first life," I say as I touch the nearest tree. As my fingers trace the crevices of the bark, it's as though my mind has no control over what my body does next. It's a remembering in my soul as I walk up to the next tree and place the palm of my hand on its center. A beaming white light appears directly in front of us as a strong wind whirls around my hair. I squint, trying to see what I had just done, but the light is too blinding. It only lasts a second before subsiding completely.

I blink a few times, bringing into focus a large cottage. I let out a small laugh as I take in its beauty. Even in the blackness of the night, I can make out its structure. It's a two-story cottage made entirely of stone. A stone pathway leads right to the door with flower beds on either side. Flowers and herbs of all kinds scurry neatly around the entirety of the cottage. Through the windows, I can see a warm glow from a fire. It feels more like home than any I'd ever had.

Vincent is behind me now as he wraps his arms around me, his hands falling gently to the center of my stomach. "I knew you'd know what to do," he says, his breath teasing against my ear, sending chills down my arms.

"I almost remember it, like it has always belonged to me," I whisper.

"It has always been ours, Ren. It's just been a few hundred years since we've last seen it."

"Ours?" I ask, cocking my head to the side to look at him.

"Mm-hmm," he nods. "We lived here together in our first life. This was the place we made to spend our lives together. But then..." He trails off, and I can feel his heartbeat quickening against my back.

Images of the day we were killed come flooding back into my mind as a tear slid down my cheek. "We were to be married that day, weren't we?" I ask, my voice faltering as I choke back more tears.

"Yes," he says, pulling me in tighter. He rests his lips on my shoulder as he lets out a shaky breath.

I turn around to face him, our bodies still pressed tightly together. "It has happened so many times before. Why should we think it'll be any different this time?" I ask as the anxiety begins to build inside me. The thought of losing him again threatens bile to rise to my throat. I couldn't watch him die again. The faint memory that was given to me was entirely too painful on its own. I couldn't have it happen all over again.

"We're prepared this time. The first time it happened, we didn't know Celest was as bad as she is. We knew uniting would bring us immense power and that we could take down any threats with that power. We just didn't know Celest felt she was one of them."

"She hasn't always been like this?" I ask.

Vincent shakes his head. "No. She was, in fact, a loving and devoted mother. But as the years went on, she became hungry with power. Knowing that our power would exceed hers... well, she was consumed with greed until she eventually grew dark. She knew we could kill her if we had to. So, she put a stop to it."

It takes me a moment to comprehend what I've just been told. Celest was at one time a good and loving mother to me. It's a thought I can hardly grasp. Knowing her now, I would have never believed it.

"We didn't know of her hatred when we were to be married?"

"No, we didn't. She acted as though she was still a loving mother. She helped you with the preparations for the ceremony. She even treated me like a son, or so I've been told by Redrich. But it was all an act. The day of our ceremony, it came as a shock to us to know she had turned against us. We never saw it coming."

I let out a shaky breath as I think of how we must have felt to learn of her betrayal. To think she was a mother that I loved and to see her plunge a stake through Vincent's heart. We never saw it coming, so of course we weren't prepared to fight her. But a sense of happiness washes over me, too. I was worried that maybe the only reason our souls were meant to join together was to take down Celest. Because we were only meant to fulfill a duty. But that isn't true anymore. We're meant to be together despite Celest.

The inside of the cottage is just as magnificent as I imagined it would be. Walking through the door, a large fireplace is lit with a black cauldron hanging above it. Hanging on the wall next to it are all kinds of cooking utensils, and a shelf nearby is stacked full of different types of herbs and spices. On the floor just in front of the fireplace lay an oval rug with chairs on either side. To the left of the front door is a dining area with a large table that could seat at least ten people. And in the middle of the room is a staircase leading to the second floor, which I imagined was where our bedchambers are.

I take a deep breath, savoring the scent of rosemary and sage as I smiled fondly.

"Are you tired?" Vincent asks. Passion burning deep in his eyes as he watches me, and my stomach responds instantly, fluttering with excitement.

I nod, wrapping my arms around his neck. "Very," I say with a yawn.

He responds by lifting me off the ground until I'm cradled in his arms. I rest my head on his shoulder as he carries me up the small steps and into one of the rooms at the far end of the hallway. Inside, I can feel a cool breeze sweeping across my face, and as I look over, I see the window cracked open.

Through each delicate motion of the white curtain against the breeze, I can see the moon full and happy in the sky as it peers in at us. I feel my soul become happier and lighter as I take in my surroundings. This is where it belongs. This is where we belong. And I vow to myself in this moment that nothing, not even Celest, could stop us this time.

I crawl into the oversized bed, letting myself sink deep under the blankets. Vincent is quickly at my side as we lay together in the peaceful silence of our surroundings. I quickly find, though, that being this close to him as we lay completely alone together, the hammering in my soul has other plans than sleep. The intensity of the vibration thrumming through my veins causes my skin to flush as a subtle ache in my core begs to be heard.

It isn't until I feel the erratic beating of Vincent's heart against me that I realize he's feeling the same way. I lock my eyes with his as he puts a hand on the small of my back, pulling me closer. Our bodies melted together, and I could swear my soul is reaching out to be with his.

Knowing what I know now, resisting him is going to be near impossible.

"Serenity," Vincent whispers, his breath playing at my lips, sending shivers down my spine.

I kiss him deeply in response, getting lost entirely in the feel of his flesh against mine. I manage to reign myself in just long enough to stop, taking a deep breath to calm the ever-growing excitement building within me.

He lets out a soft chuckle as he nuzzles into the nape of my neck. "Just think of it this way; Redrich is keeping a close eye on us. He'll know if we go too far," Vincent says.

The thought immediately knocks me down a few pegs. Redrich was very much aware the last time we went too far, which can only mean he can somehow sense what we're doing. Thinking back to the night in the tent, his voice sounded like he was right there in the room with us. The very thought of that being the case is enough for all the erotic excitement to leave my body.

Thank the Gods for small miracles.

"You sure do know how to seduce a girl," I say with a huff, trying to regain my composure.

Vincent's mouth curves in a devilish smirk as he tucks the loose hair behind my ear. "Trust me, love. What you're feeling now is nothing compared to what you'll be feeling when I do seduce you."

My stomach flips wildly as his eyes pierce into mine. Making me any more excited than I already have been seems impossible. But I couldn't wait to take him up on his challenge.

"I'll be counting on it," I say, kissing him once more, letting the warmth of his lips linger a moment longer.

As I let go, he gives me a soft smile, but his eyes have a look of concern as he watches me closely. "Ren, if this wasn't needed to be rid of Celest, would you still want to marry me?" he asks, his voice tinged with vulnerability.

My heart hammers loudly in my chest as I sit up on my elbow. "I wouldn't care if there were a thousand other ways to be rid of her, I'd still choose you. I have chosen you in this lifetime and all the others," I say, caressing his cheek with my thumb. "I even chose you in another realm when I didn't know if you even existed."

He gives a relieved smile as he wraps his arm around my waist. "I just needed to be sure that we're doing this because you want to and not because you have to."

"Are you doing it because you want to?" I ask, suddenly becoming all too aware of the fact that maybe he's only doing this because he feels like he has to.

I know he can feel the anxiety growing in me, for I could also feel the anxiety in him before he asked me. He quickly positions himself, so he's now propped up on his elbow, our eyes locked together. And he speaks now as if he has read my mind. "Don't ever think I want you only to gain power over Celest. I've wanted you since the day I met you eight hundred years ago before we knew anything about this. My love for you has only grown stronger with each passing day, Ren." He stops for a moment before speaking in a low, husky tone. "My soul belongs to you."

I let out a shaky breath as I wrap my arm around his side. "And my soul belongs to you. Always." I can feel the hot tears stinging my eyes as they slide down my cheeks. Vincent quickly brushes them away with his thumb as he kisses my forehead. I let myself fall into his touch for a long moment, savoring every second we have together. Being away from him for so long left me feeling weak and vulnerable. I know now that that was the best form of punishment Celest could cast upon us. Who needed death when you could just as easily rip the other half of your soul away, leaving you feeling empty and helpless in a never-ending cycle of torture?

I try not to think too much more of the pain I have felt for so long as I lie next to Vincent. I focus on the feeling of our bodies pressed together, his lips resting lightly on my forehead as I finally drift into the kind of peaceful sleep I've been longing for, for the past twenty-eight years. The rhythm of his breathing and the warmth of his embrace lull me into a state of contentment, and I hold onto the hope that this time, we can complete the ceremony our souls were always meant for.

Chapter 23

A voice in my head jolts me awake. I frantically sit up in bed and glance around the room. The sun has begun to rise, its rays peeking through the trees and casting a soft glow onto the bed. I listen again, waiting for the voice I had just heard. It sounded so familiar, but I couldn't be sure to whom it belonged. The only thing I hear now is the steady rhythm of Vincent's breathing. I glance over at him, still sleeping soundly. It couldn't have been him who called out to me. In fact, it sounded more like a woman's voice.

I rub the drowsiness from my eyes, convincing myself that it had been nothing more than a dream. I lie back down next to Vincent, nestling closely to his chest as he instinctively wraps his arm tighter around my waist. Just as I'm drifting off, I hear it again. My eyes pop open as I wait in anticipation. This time I have no doubt about what I heard. Her voice is so clear to me now.

"Ren! Are you going to leave me out here waiting? I'm dying to see you!"

"Oh, my Gods!" I exclaim, sprinting out of bed and down the hallway.

"Ren, what is it?" Vincent calls after me as I run down the stairs, but I'm far too excited to answer him.

I open the door and stop in my tracks as emotions begin to rise within me. I hadn't realized until this moment exactly how much I have missed her.

"Arian," I breathe. "Oh, Arian, I've missed you so much!" I say, tackling her with a hug.

She lets out a soft sob against my ear as she clings tightly to me. "I can't believe you're really here. I didn't know if I'd ever see you again."

"How did you know I was back?" I ask as I let go of her.

She narrows her eyes, giving me a smirk. "I'm a seer, remember? As soon as I saw that you were back, I had to come to you. Redrich told me where to find you."

I nod, remembering that the last time I saw her, she was just discovering her gifts. I take in her small frame, her slim and delicate facial features, and realize a lot has changed about her. She's no longer a servant to a powerful kingdom, for she now has her own power. Her demeanor is no longer shy and nervous like she once portrayed herself. Now, she has the look of a fierce and wild soul in her eyes, but in a way that would make most envious. She's very much found her way in this world in the years that I've been gone. She's found where she belongs and who she really is, and it shines brightly in every aspect of her being.

And it makes me realize something about myself. I, too, used to be a shy and nervous girl, barely making it day by day with the fear of Celest looming over us like a dark cloud, never knowing when she might strike us down for whatever purpose suited her on that day. I have only recently discovered the strong powers I possess, and I realize how much it, and all the events leading up to this moment, has changed me. Especially since, for the past three decades, Celest had erased all memories of who I really was, leading me to believe I was a powerless, pathetic girl in a world that wasn't mine. But now, finding out what I have about myself since returning, I no longer feel that way. I know now that I'm an ancient Mirgorist sent by the universe with Vincent at my side to be what we truly are. Not only are we the only force known to take down even the most powerful of sorcerers, but we're also much more than that.

We're a force of love that has never been written about before. We're a mystery that only the beginning of time can comprehend.

"Yes, I—" My response is cut short as I look into her eyes. They've glazed over, and there's nothing to them but white staring back at me. Her body is perfectly still, unresponsive to my touch as I grip her arm.

"Arian?" I ask, panic gripping my chest. But she doesn't respond.

"What's wrong with her?" Vincent asks as he walks up to us.

"I don't know!" I say, turning back to her. "Arian, can you hear me?" I ask, shaking her.

"Yes, yes, I can hear you," she says. Her eyes remain white for a second longer before flicking back to their normal state.

"What the hell was that?" I ask. Arian doesn't seem concerned at all about what had just happened, confusing me even more.

"I'll explain that later. For now, we have to get inside. Celest is close," she says as she quickly makes her way through the door.

My heart picks up pace at the mention of Celest. She's close, meaning she's back in this realm, hunting us once more.

We follow her into the house and quickly shut the door, the warding spell immediately taking over to cloak the house. She couldn't find us now, could she?

"How do you know she's close?" I ask.

"I saw her," Arian says as she sits at the small table in the kitchen.

“How did you see her?” I ask.

“Much has changed with me since we last saw one another, Ren. After you were gone, I felt I needed to know more about myself. I needed to know if there was anything I could do to bring you back. That’s when I met Redrich. He taught me all I needed to know about myself. That’s when I learned I can leave my body to check my surroundings without being seen. That’s how I know Celest is close.”

I stay silent for a long moment, trying to take it all in. Just a couple of days ago, I was mostly convinced I was losing my mind, and I certainly didn't think magical beings existed. That I am a magical being. When the memories of my life in this land that were forced from my memory came flooding back into my mind, I couldn't help but feel overwhelmed. I now have two separate lives living inside of me. And to have so many of the answers I desperately searched for before I was forced from this land, well, it's all a bit much to take in all at once.

"Ren, are you alright?" Vincent asks, touching my arm. The electric current coursing through me from his touch snaps me viciously from my thoughts.

"Yes, fine," I say, though I am far from it. "Celest is back," I look to Arian now.

Her face hardens as Celest's name spills from my lips. "Yes. She's close," Arian says, her eyes turning white once more.

She's gone only briefly before her eyes return to normal. "She can feel the magic protecting the house, but she can't find us. Though it isn't stopping her from trying," Arian says.

My blood runs cold as I stand from my chair. I slowly walk over to the window, peering out through the sheer curtain. I don't see anything as I scan the area. Nothing but the trees that surround us. In the daylight, I can now see a stream flowing softly over smooth rocks, small ripples forming at the bottom. I didn't notice in the dark of the night when we first arrived, but everything seems alive. Not just the trees or the forest floor we saw glowing brightly. The water too is alive in its own majestic way as it dances and bubbles happily down the hill.

"I don't see her now," I say. "She must have…" My words are cut short as I let out a gasp. I can feel the energy draining from my body as my blood begins to flow with daggers of ice, its sharp edges cutting me raw. The room stays deathly silent, for I know Vincent and Arian are both seeing exactly what I am. Seemingly out of nowhere, Celest is directly on the other side of the window. Her eyes, looking as though they were conjured by the devil himself, are staring directly at me.

My heart pounds violently in my chest as I stare back at her, not daring to move. It's only now that I take a long look at her features. Her brown eyes are wild with hate, small creases forming on either side. Her pale skin glows radiantly as if she isn't an ancient, evil being. Her red hair is placed in a sloppy bun on top of her head, strands of hair poking out every which way. I know she's a woman on a mission, for she would never think of looking so unkempt before.

"Don't worry, she can't see us or hear us," Arian says. "But she is feeling your presence. She knows you're here."

I quickly back away, Vincent coming quickly to me as he puts a protective hand on my shoulder as I sit back down, my eyes not leaving Celest once. I fear if I turn my back to her, she'll plunge a stake through my chest like she has done before.

Finally, my presence must begin to fade, for she quickly turns away, cursing under her breath. "I will find you, you filthy child. Mark my words."

It isn't until she's completely out of sight that I realize I've been holding my breath. Dizziness washes over me in waves, making my mind hazy. I take a breath, trying to calm my jittering nerves. Vincent quickly places his hand on mine, sensing the presence of my ever-growing anxiety. Once again, the warmth his touch puts me at ease.

"Now she knows where we are. It isn't safe for us to stay here even if she can't see us. She'll find a way. She always does," I say, feeling the anger growing deep within me.

"That's why the ceremony must begin tonight." I jump almost out of my chair as Redrich says the words right next to me, Uncle standing closely by his side.

"Christ!" I exclaim, quickly standing.

Redrich gives a perplexed look. "Christ?" He says the word slowly as if trying to piece together its meaning. And that's when it hits me. He doesn't know.

I can't help but smile at his confused expression. "It's an expression used in the other realm. Actually, it's considered bad as it's taking the Lord's name in vain."

"The Lord?" Uncle asks, looking equally as confused as Redrich.

"Yes. It... Never mind," I say with a wave of my hand. Now is no time for a lesson on other realms. "How did the two of you get in here?" I ask.

"You gave me permission many years ago in the event of an emergency," Redrich says.

"Oh... of course," I say with a nod.

"The ceremony must be completed tonight if we are to have any chance of defeating Celest. She knows where you are now, and as you said, it's only a matter of time before she figures out how to take down the cloaking spell," Redrich says.

I nod slowly. This should be the most exciting day of my life as I get to be forever united with the man I love. But I only feel the ever-growing presence of fear as memories of our first ceremony flash through my mind.

"What is it, Ren?" Uncle asks.

"It's just... should we wait? Celest was just here. She's going to be close. She sensed me, and she won't leave this place until I'm found," I say, the bile rising rapidly to my throat.

Redrich purses his lips as he draws nearer to me. "Serenity, my dear, I think it's time you meet someone," he says, glancing toward the door.

Chapter 24

I quickly turn to face the door, nervous anticipation rising within me. There, standing in the doorway, is a middle-aged man, regal and strong. His dark hair is cut short, and his brown eyes gleam happily as they smile at me. This is the same man I saw from the memories Redrich showed me, the man I loved dearly.

"It's you," I say cautiously. "The man from my memories."

He slowly makes his way over to me, clasping both my hands in his. Love and a hint of sadness cloud his eyes. "Yes, my darling. I'm your father."

The breath quickly leaves my lungs as I take an unsteady step back. My father? How could this be? My father is dead.

"But you died! You died in battle when I was a small child!" I stammer, my mind reeling.

He gives a soft smile as he puts a gentle hand on my shoulder. "I had to fake my death so Celest wouldn't catch on to what I was up to. I knew I had to find a way to keep you and Vincent alive long enough for you to finally meet once more. If Celest had known what I was planning, she would have killed you both long before I had the chance to cast my protection spell."

My head spins as I try to take this all in. My father has been alive this whole time, hiding in the shadows, keeping us safe from a distance. My entire life, well, the entirety of this life, I have always felt a deep yearning for my father. I have always wondered what he was like, and if I was anything like him, for I am nothing like Celest.

I shake my head, urging the dizziness to subside as I catch my breath. I can think of nothing to say as tears begin to slip from my eyes and flow rapidly down my cheeks. The only thing I can do now is wrap my arms around him as I sob softly against him. My father. The feeling I have with his arms wrapped protectively around me as he soothes my breathless sobs is a feeling of familiarity. It's a feeling I know so well, and I can only assume it's previous memories of him creeping to the surface.

"Oh, my love, it's okay now," he says in a soothing voice. "I have found my way back to you once more."

"I've missed you so," I say as I pull back to look up at him.

"I've missed you too, my darling. I'm sorry I had to stay away for so long."

I can feel the strong familiar current of Vincent standing next to me. I snap myself from the shock of finally meeting my father as I turn to look at him. Vincent is staring at him as if he has missed him just as much as I have. He too must feel the familiar pull of the man standing before us.

"Oh, my boy," my father says as he wraps Vincent in a tight hug. "It is so wonderful to finally have us all together again. It's just as it was eight hundred years ago. Though it feels like only yesterday."

"How is it that I feel so much like I know you, but have no memory of you?" Vincent asks. It's the same question that has been gnawing at me.

"That will come in time. For both of you," he says, looking between us. "Once the ceremony is complete, you'll remember everything."

The deepening pit in my stomach returns brutally. The happiness of meeting my father has been struck down by the ugly truth. Celest will stop at nothing until she catches us.

"Father, why must the ceremony happen today? Celest will surely find us and do everything in her power to put a stop to it," I say.

He stays silent for a moment, looking between Uncle Edmond and Redrich before finally looking back to me. "I asked them not to say anything because I didn't want you to worry. But I think it's time you know."

"Know what?" Vincent asks, clasping my hand. I can feel his worry as if it were my own. But maybe that's because I am just as worried as he. Something has been kept from us. Something big.

"When I cast the protection spell upon the two of you, there was a catch, just like with most magic. You are only protected against Celest until midnight tomorrow when the moon is at its highest point in the sky. If you aren't united by then, there is nothing stopping Celest from killing you both," my father says.

When neither of us responds, he continues, "Twenty-eight years should have been plenty of time for the ceremony. But I never anticipated Celest casting you away for all those years. I knew once the two of you met, the beginning of the ceremony would happen rapidly."

"How…" My words come out in a croak, so I clear my throat before beginning again. "How is it possible that Vincent and I met in this life? Why didn't Celest send him away the first day he came to Duix?" I had always wondered why she ordered me to stay away from him. Why she stressed over what I was doing or where I was every minute of the day when she could have just as easily had Vincent leave. Then she would never have to worry.

Father smiles. "The protection spell wasn't just to keep you safe; it was to keep you together. As fate would have it, Celest had no choice but to keep Vincent near. She didn't know why, but there was a strong force preventing her from sending him away. Just as she didn't know why she couldn't have you killed as a young girl. Though she tried many times."

My blood runs cold. Celest has tried killing me many times. I think back to all the times I was sick as a child, bedridden for weeks at a time, the physician never pinpointing exactly what caused it, though he suspected poison was at play. Celest put on a good show, demanding whoever was behind the attacks on her daughter be caught and reprimanded. What a wonderful actress she was.

I clear my throat as I begin to speak. “How will we pull this off? Maybe we can just do the ceremony here?” I ask. I see no other way for this to happen other than in the protective cloak that masks this house. Otherwise, we would surely be found, and who knew what Celest would do then.

“The ceremony must be performed at the Isle of Alba,” Redrich chimes in.

“The Isle of Alba?” I ask. I try to recall a time that I might have heard that name in the past, but nothing comes to me. Though I have no recollection of the name, the familiar current that courses through my veins burns hot as the words fall from my lips. It’s an awakening like no other as I feel the power churning just beneath the surface, demanding to be set free, urging me to remember who I am and why I’m here. Not only that, but I feel another familiar pull with the same urgency of power that has filled me completely.

Vincent and I lock eyes as the energy between us begins to grow and run rampant. The same sharp ice that filled our veins when we first arrived at the City of Myria begins to take over completely.

The world around me goes hazy as the light dims from my eyes. I can hear Arian yelling something as she runs over to Vincent and me, but it’s too muffled to make out. The pain is too strong as I try desperately to take back control of my body. Redrich places his hands on my and Vincent's foreheads as he did when we first arrived at the castle in an attempt to place a spell on us so the pain crashing through us might subside. But this time, nothing happens. Vincent and I clasp our hands together, though I can't feel his hand in mine, only what feels like icy shards ripping through me as we both collapse to the floor. I try desperately to speak, to tell someone to help us, but the words won't escape my lips. I stare into Vincent's eyes as I feel the life draining from me. If this is how I must leave this world again, at least the last person I see will be him. I blink a tear away and Vincent gives me a sad smile.

The world goes black around me, the frantic muffled voices becoming void in the darkness that surrounds us. Peace washes over me in warm waves, thawing the icy feeling from my body.

Before I can savor the feeling of warmth any longer, unconsciousness puts its strong grip on me completely.

Chapter 25

Dark, churning clouds hovered ominously, threatening a grand storm. The wind whipped fiercely as two figures made their way into the forest of Alba, finally stopping only once they were safe from the growing storm under a large oak tree. Its low-hanging branches protected them from the rain that now pounded down with force.

"We can't keep going like this," Valentina said, her voice strained with urgency. "We must do something quickly."

Thaddeus nodded in agreement. "When we created this world, we could have never anticipated this."

Valentina paced under the large tree, her mind racing with possible solutions. Together, she, the goddess of love, and Thaddeus, the god of peace, had created a world of magic—a place of peace, love, and acceptance for all who entered. It had been a dream of theirs for many centuries, and finally, they had made it happen. But now, the world they created had been overrun by evil forces that threatened to tear apart all they had worked so hard for. The peaceful, happy souls who inhabited this land had been brutally struck down by the evil gods and goddesses, who hoped to claim this world as their own. Valentina and Thaddeus fought with all the power they had within themselves to save their precious creation, and it almost killed them both. Being a god or goddess didn't mean they were entirely invincible to all other entities that lurked in the dark. There were many powerful beings that roamed—many that were just as strong, maybe even stronger, than they were. But together, they were able to defeat all that threatened them, though not before the slaughter of most of their creation.

And they both knew it was only a matter of time before some other powerful being would come back to destroy this land and all who resided here once more.

"I have an idea," Valentina finally said, stopping her pacing.

"What is it?" Thaddeus asked, his undivided attention on her.

"We create a being that's never been before. One that's so powerful, nothing can defeat it."

Thaddeus contemplated this information, beginning to pace. Finally, he stopped abruptly and faced his goddess. A sly smile beamed on his face. "What's the strongest force to exist? One that can never be broken or swayed?" he asked.

Valentina let out an excited laugh, beaming at him. "Love," she said. As the goddess of love herself, she knew exactly how powerful it was. It was untouchable even to the most powerful of beings.

Love was a mysterious force that could not be tamed. It was untouchable.

"Right," Thaddeus smiled. "So, we create two beings."

"Two beings with one soul," Valentina said, her excitement growing wild. Love was her domain, and this would be her greatest creation yet.

"Yes," Thaddeus nodded. "But how? How do we create two beings with only one soul?"

Valentina drew closer to her god and lover, placing a hand on his cheek. She stared into his loving eyes, savoring every moment, memorizing every detail of his features. "There's only one way," she finally said, sadness filling her tone.

"What is it, darling?" he asked, placing a soft hand on her shoulder.

"To create something this powerful, something more powerful than even we are, we must die," she said.

Thaddeus scanned her eyes as tears quickly threatened to well in his. "Is there no other way?" he asked.

Valentina shook her head. "There is no other way. But fear not. Once the ceremony is complete, our two souls will forever be intertwined together, as one. We will never be apart, my darling."

The god of peace didn't need to consider it for long. For he was peace, and she was love. Together, they would create exactly that. The land they worked so hard to build would finally be safe from all who sought to destroy it.

"Then that is what we shall do," he said softly.

Together, in a blissful state of peace and love, they shared their bodies under the now clearing sky. The moon shone brightly on their bare flesh as they explored each other tenderly for the last time.

Now, they lay under the shimmering stars, wrapped tightly in each other's arms.

"I love you, my darling. I'll meet you on the other side," Valentina said, still breathless from their time together.

"I love you," Thaddeus said. "My soul is forever yours."

Before another word could be said between them, their bodies faded away into the soft soil. A tall, regal tree sprouted freely from the ground in their place. It was there, in the black of the night, that their two souls shone brightly as they danced around the tree, finally joining as one. It was here where they would stay until the day came that their new creation must come to life to save this world of love and peace. It was here where a new god and goddess would join in a love so strong, not even the goddess of love herself could comprehend.

It was here where it all began.

Chapter 26

"Ren?" I hear my name called in a muffled tone.

It takes me a moment to realize that I'm no longer in the forest with the god of peace and the goddess of love. The vision I had of them was so real that I could feel everything they felt. I could smell everything they smelled, the rain pelting violently on my skin as the storm rolled in, the dampening moss stirring up its aroma.

Finally, I open my eyes, seeing Vincent sitting upright next to me, rubbing his eyes. He looks pale, like death had its grip on him for only a moment before showing mercy and letting him go. I knew then he had experienced the same vision I had. I sit up with him, my head spinning wildly for a moment, the world around me seeming fuzzy and unreal, as if I've stepped into unknown territory.

"Are you okay?" my father asks, a worried look crossing his face.

"I- I think so," is all I can manage to say.

"What the hell was that?" Vincent asks.

I shake my head, still unable to fully comprehend the world around me. This was nothing like the other dreams or visions I have had in the past. The others felt real, and I knew there was something more to them than just being dreams. But this… this was something different entirely. I felt every emotion Valentina and Thaddeus felt. I had a sense that I knew them personally. The magic I felt was like nothing I've ever experienced before. It was all-knowing, all-powerful.

"What did you see?" Redrich asks, looking between Vincent and me.

"It's going to sound crazy," I begin. "But I saw a couple. Thaddeus, the god of peace, and Valentina, the goddess of love. They had just won a great war. Evil filled their lands, mangling their people, attempting to take over the world they created. They created two beings so powerful that nothing could destroy them. But in creating them, they had to die." Saying it out loud just now sounded mad.

"Two powerful beings… with one soul," Vincent says as we lock eyes.

The breath catches in my lungs as I realize what he's saying. Redrich has told us that our souls are meant to be one. Once united, we'll be powerful enough to destroy Celest. Could it be that Vincent and I watched ourselves be created?

The room remains silent for a beat. Redrich's face lights up as if he had just witnessed a miracle. "How remarkable!" he exclaims.

"What is?" I ask, waiting for him to confirm what I already suspected.

"There's much I didn't get a chance to tell you before the spell wore off the last we spoke in the castle. There's much that none of you in this room know," he says.

"Well, we'd love to hear it now," Uncle Edmond says, drawing closer.

"You weren't just created by an unknown entity. You were created by two of the most powerful beings ever known. The god of peace and the goddess of love. The two of them combined created a force so powerful, so… terrifying that none dared to cross them. None until that time in history when their enemies tried taking over their world. They realized then that they weren't indestructible, for they were almost killed." Redrich stops for a moment to look between Vincent and me, smiling with pride. "That's when they created you."

Suspecting it was true was nothing compared to the feeling of knowing it was true. I stay silent, taking it all in. Only remembering this life and none of the others before was hard enough. But to find out Vincent and I are ancient beings created by a god and goddess; it is far too much to take in. My powers have been steadily growing, that much is true. But I most certainly did not feel strong enough to be created by such powerful beings as Thaddeus and Valentina.

"You mean we saw our… our creation?" Vincent asks.

Redrich nods. "Yes, yes, you saw how it all began," he says breathlessly.

"What are we?" I blurt out.

"You're a goddess, my dear," Redrich says.

I let out a nervous laugh. Me. A goddess. None of this seemed at all possible. It wasn't too long ago I was just a young woman in the state of Maine, in an entirely different realm, barely making it through each day because I was convinced I was going insane. And now I'm being told I'm a goddess.

"A goddess?" I ask, suspicion filling my tone.

"Indeed. Just as Vincent is a god."

I stand now, pacing back and forth. I abruptly stop to look back at Redrich. "The god and goddess of what?" I ask.

He shakes his head. "You aren't just a god and a goddess; you are *the* god and goddess. You are one. A universal anomaly, just as Thaddeus and Valentina planned. No one can possibly begin to describe exactly what the two of you are, for there is no word for the power that resides within you. They created one soul for two bodies. One all-powerful soul that was split during your creation. It is why your powers aren't as strong as they should be. It's why Celest is so terrified of you completing the ceremony. And it is why it must be done now."

I find the nearest chair and sit back hard, my legs suddenly feeling like they may fail me if I were to stand any longer. Not just a goddess. But one so powerful there is no word for what I really am. Suddenly, I want no one in the room with me. Only Vincent.

"I need you all to leave. I need to be alone with Vincent," I say firmly. He is the only one who can calm the storm that's raging inside of me now. The only one who can bring peace to my heart. Which all makes sense now, as the god of peace is part of the reason why we're here.

Redrich gives one quick nod. "Certainly. We'll be back at the castle. I'll come back for you in one hour. That is all the time I can give you."

"I understand," I say, but when I go to look over at them, the room is already empty except for Vincent and me.

Finally, I let out the shaky breath I've been holding this whole time. I stand and make my way over to Vincent, his arms instantly wrapping tightly around me. I breathe him in, concentrating on the power that surges through me at his touch. It's a calming feeling that I have grown so fond of.

It's a feeling that no longer startles me like it did so long ago. Now, I crave it. I need it.

"I always knew you were a goddess," Vincent whispers, his lips teasing my ear.

"How?" I say with a smile, looking up at him.

"One look at you tells everyone all they need to know," he says, caressing my cheek.

"Well, Sir Vincent. If that's the case, you must be the god of all gods," I say with a sly smile.

"Apparently, I am," he replies.

My heartbeat quickens. Yes, he really is the god of all gods. We both are. The very thought of us being all-powerful together, as one, sends my need for him into overdrive. It's stronger than it has ever been as our eyes lock, both knowing what the other is feeling. I can feel the arousal coursing through him, just as he can feel it in me. I need this man, this god, so much it makes my entire body ache.

"Vincent..." I murmur as I wrap my arms around his neck. Nothing more needs to be said as our lips meet with urgency. The power vibrating between us grows stronger with each caress as his hands travel lower, trailing along the curves of my body. I let out a soft moan as he finally stops at my waist, pulling me closer to him with force. His other hand travels up to the nape of my neck as we kiss with such passion, I'm convinced the whole room may catch fire.

"I need you right now," I say breathlessly. The magnificent god that stands before me gives a smile conjured by the devil himself as his lips make their way to my neck, his tongue trailing slowly up to my ear as he playfully bites at the lobe. I let out a breath as I grip his hair between my hands, savoring every kiss and flick of his tongue. But I need more. I need all of him. My very soul demands it. "Please..." I beg. I can't possibly handle this wonderful torture for one more minute.

Vincent pulls back, looking at me, his breath quick and short as he needs me just as much as I need him. The burning desire in his eyes as he looks at me turns me on all over again. He's like a wild animal, and I can think of no better way to tame his animalistic instincts than to have him right here and now on this table.

"Right here on the table, huh?" he says with a sly smile, reading my thoughts.

I'm shocked for a moment, but it should come as no surprise, for I'm reading his thoughts too. As much as he wants me, he also wants this to be right. The ceremony needs to be completed before we can go any further. The cursed ceremony that is stopping me from having him now.

"The table seems like a perfect place to me," I say.

He kisses me again for one hot second before saying, "We need to do this ceremony. Now. My soul can't handle not having you for a second longer."

"I quite agree. This ceremony does need to happen now," Redrich says, standing right next to us.

I jump, a small scream escaping my lips. "You have got to stop doing that! You'll make my heart give out before we can even complete the ceremony," I scold.

"I thought it would be safe leaving the two of you alone for an hour, but I see I was wrong. There will be no more alone time until the ceremony begins," Redrich says.

I cross my arms, scowling at him. "Are you scolding a goddess?" I ask.

His lips twitch as he tries to hold back a smile. "Yes, I am. Now let's go," he says.

I turn back to Vincent, who is now holding back a laugh of his own. He puts an arm around my waist, pulling me close and whispering in my ear. "I'll fulfill all of your wildest desires soon, my lady." The very thought sends me spiraling over the edge of ecstasy once more.

Redrich clears his throat. “Now,” he says in a stern voice.

I let out a frustrated huff and walk over to him, placing our hands on his arm. In a bright flash, the cabin disappears around us as we float through time and space to our next destination. To the place where it all began. The place where our souls will finally be united.

Chapter 27

Before I have time to even blink, we are back at the castle. Father, Uncle, and Arian are sitting in Redrich's office, talking among themselves as we enter. I'm still dizzy from the adrenaline of the magic that brought us here and the arousal that is still pulsating through me at full force. I feel as if my brain has gone haywire, and nothing will stop it until I have Vincent.

Arian has a sly grin smeared across her face as she clears her throat. "I didn't realize an all-powerful god and goddess could possibly get in trouble with anyone. But you managed it," she says.

My face turns hot as I realize everyone in the room knows why Redrich brought us back so early. A quick realization comes to me as I snap my head back up to Arian. "You spied on us!" I accuse.

Arian shrugs her shoulders, giving me an innocent smile. "Guilty," she says.

"And here I thought we were friends," I say in a teasing tone.

Father clears his throat as he steps towards us. "We must get to the Isle of Alba as quickly as possible. I can feel Celest. She is close."

I give a quick nod as I reach for Vincent's hand. I may be a goddess, but that doesn't mean I don't feel fear like everyone else. And right now, it's boiling hot inside of me. We don't have long before Father's protection spell comes to an end. We'll soon be vulnerable to Celest's wrath. If we don't get to the Isle of Alba soon, she could stop us indefinitely. Thaddeus and Valentina's deaths would have been for nothing. And that is something I cannot allow to happen.

The sun has faded beneath the horizon as the moon shines brightly upon us when we reach the Isle of Alba. Redrich used his magic to get us here quickly and safely. And now, the time has finally come to complete the ceremony. As we step foot on the island, a strange sense washes over me like I've been here before. The magic now flowing through me feels familiar and strong. It feels like it has always belonged to me. To us. The vibration in my veins intensifies with each step closer to the Tree of Alba. The deep longing and primal need for Vincent grows just as out of control. As he clasps my hand in his, I can feel the ecstasy surging through him in a powerful wave. Our eyes lock for one long, intense moment, our hearts beating like war drums in rhythm with one another. I have to focus all of my attention on breathing in this moment, so I don't give way to the intense emotions that are threatening to completely take hold.

"We're almost there," Redrich says, and I finally feel myself relaxing. We have made it here. Now all we must do is complete the ceremony.

We round a corner, deep in the forest. Its luminescent glow is strong as it hums against my skin. The forest floor and the trees alike are speaking to me and Vincent in a language only we can understand. It is welcoming us home.

I can just barely make it out, but just ahead is a large and regal tree, standing tall and proud as it hums in tune with every beat of our hearts. And I know, this is where it all began. Where we were created, and where we will now be united.

Father stops abruptly, and I crash into his back. "We have a problem," he says. The growing anxiety in his voice sends me on high alert as I scan the area.

"Hello, my darling." The voice sends chills down my spine as I turn to look at her.

"Celest," I say in a threatening tone. "What are you…"

I can't finish the sentence, for my body has frozen just as it had the night in the cave with Vincent. Just as it had right before I was banished from this world.

"No," I finally say. "No, you can't do this."

"It's already done. Say goodbye to your beloved, for you will never see him again," she says with a smile that sends a chill over my body.

I look over at Vincent, unable to speak once more as the tears roll down my cheeks. His face is pale as he reaches for me, and his eyes are full of rage and desperation. I reach my hand up, just barely grasping his hand before falling backward. I never hit the ground though, for I keep falling into an endless darkness. I let out a scream, but nothing happens. The darkness that is taking hold is suffocating me completely. As I close my eyes, I can hear Arian screaming in a rage I have never heard from her before. The ground above me shakes as Vincent lets out a rush of power towards Celest. But it isn't enough. Not without me. Not without the ceremony being completed.

I feel my heart break as I begin to lose consciousness. I've lost my love once more. This time, I'm not sure I'll ever get him back.

Chapter 28

My ears ring loudly, jolting me back to consciousness. As I open my eyes, the sun pierces into them brightly. Above me, I see a tree, familiar to me as I've seen it many times before. I jolt up, suddenly realizing where I am.

"Ren? Oh, my God, Ren!"

My breath catches as I hear her voice. I quickly turn in her direction, seeing her running towards me from the house.

"Mom," I say in a small breath.

She quickly reaches me, falling to the ground at my side as she sobs into my shoulder. "Ren, my girl," she cries. "I didn't think I'd ever see you again."

I pull away to look at her, tears streaming down my face. "I've missed you so much, Momma. I'm sorry I had to leave you," I say.

The realization suddenly hits me. I did leave her, but now here she is, in front of me once more. I have been sent back to this world. I've been cast away from my world and into a place that doesn't belong to me. I shake my head as I look around. The house I lived in for most of my life while being here still stands, looking exactly as I left it. The field, with the oak tree, hasn't changed even a little.

"No," I say, shaking my head again. "No, I can't be here." My heart begins to pound fiercely in my chest as I force myself to breathe.

My mom grabs my shoulders lightly to comfort me. "How did you get here?" she asks.

"Celest," I say, anger quickly turning into a burning rage. "The ceremony. We were about to finish the ceremony when she came and banished me to this land again."

"This land?" My mom says cautiously.

"There are many worlds and many realms. I have never belonged to this one. If I don't get back by midnight, the protection spell that Father placed on us will be gone. She'll kill Vincent." I feel the bile rising in my throat as I say the last part. I cannot find out that Vincent has been killed. And it will surely happen if we don't complete our ceremony. After she's finished with him, Celest will come to this world and kill me, too.

"Ren, I don't understand..."

A groan comes from behind me, and I whip around to see what's happening. There, lying on the ground, is Uncle Edmond.

"Oh!" I say as I crawl over to him. "Uncle, how did you get here?"

Uncle groans again as he sits up. "I jumped in the void with you. I wasn't going to let you do this alone again. Vincent tried too, but..." He cuts his words short as he looks at me.

"But what?" I ask in a panic. "Uncle, what happened to Vincent?"

"Celest stopped him. But don't worry, he can't be dead, remember."

"Ren?" Mom says as she reaches us with caution.

I smile at her as I look over to Uncle. "Mom, this is..."

"Uncle Edmond," she finishes.

Uncle has a perplexed look as he glances between us. "How did you know?" he asks.

"I've had the same dreams as Ren. We shared them somehow. I've seen you so many times, I feel as if I know you. I've seen you love and protect her as if she were your own child," she says with a loving smile. "I cannot thank you enough for that."

Uncle stands as he reaches for her hand. "I have always loved her like my own, and I will continue to do so for the rest of my life, my lady," he says as he kisses her hand.

I let out a small laugh at the look of confusion she gives him. Gestures like this are very foreign in this world. Ones you see only in movies.

"As I said, this is a different world," I say, grinning at her.

"Right, yes," she says as she looks at me. "Do I bow, or...?"

I let out a loud laugh. "No, that isn't necessary."

"What happens if the ceremony isn't completed?" she asks.

I pause for a moment as I look at Uncle Edmond and then back to her. "We'll die. Either by Celest's hands or by our souls literally ripping from our bodies." I meant to give a softer explanation. I don't want her to worry. But I didn't have one. That is exactly what will happen. Just standing here now, I can feel the aching, the cry my soul is screaming out to Vincent. It won't be long now before it becomes too impatient and goes after Vincent's soul, leaving my body behind. I relax, only slightly, at the thought. Even in death, our souls will be as one. I'll never really lose him, for I am him, and he is me. But I still cannot allow that to happen. The world I was forced to leave behind is still in danger. Celest will stop at nothing to gain power over all who live there. And I was created to stop that very thing from happening. My living body is not finished here.

"I'm having a hard time wrapping my head around this," Mom says as she sways a little. Uncle Edmond quickly grabs hold of her arm, steadying her.

"We should go inside and sit as we tell your mother everything," Uncle suggests.

Uncle Edmond and I spend the next few hours going over everything we know. We start with when Vincent and I were first born into our realm, about our first life together, and how Celest killed us as we were about to begin the ceremony. We recount all the other lives after that, how our souls were created by a god and goddess to be as one. I explain how we were made to be all-powerful together, to defeat even the darkest and most cunning of beings. By the end of it, I feel exhausted. It's too much for even me to comprehend.

She stays silent for a long moment, struggling to take it all in.

"You…you're a goddess," she finally says.

"Not just any goddess," Uncle starts. "She and Vincent together are a force never before seen."

She lets out a nervous laugh. "And your father? He's alive?"

I see the sadness welling in her eyes at the mention of my father. She has always known that in this life, I missed having a father just as I did in my realm.

I clasp her hand as I nod. "Yes, he's been protecting us. And the only way for him to do that was by being away from Celest."

"And this is your last chance? There are no other lives after this?"

I shake my head. "No, this is it. Even Thaddeus and Valentina couldn't foresee this. They had no idea how powerfully our souls would demand to be together."

"And it's happening fast," Uncle says. "The pain the two of you are feeling is new. Redrich has never seen this before."

"I know," I say with a nod. "I can feel it even now, in another world. It's quite painful."

"Then what do we do? How do we get you back?" Mom asks.

"I don't know," I admit. "I guess we hope for the orb to come back for us to pass through." It's the only thing I can think of to get back. Uncle and

Vincent have done it before. Maybe now, he and Father can do it with the help of Arian and Redrich.

"Something will have to happen soon. We can't wait much longer," Uncle says. I can hear the panic in his voice, but his expression remains calm. He's right. This needs to be done soon, or all hope is lost. We only have a few hours before midnight approaches in our land. After that, there's no telling what might happen and how rapidly.

Before midnight approaches in our land. The words echo loudly in my head as a thought occurs to me.

"Mom, how long have I been gone?" I ask.

She looks at the calendar hanging on the wall and counts to herself. "About a month," she says. "I've come back here every day so I could…feel closer to you."

I give her a sad smile. I can't imagine how she has felt this whole time. For me, it has only been a few days, and I have missed her so much. A whole month without her would have been dreadful.

"This is a good thing. For me, it has only been a few days. Time goes much differently here than it does in my world."

"Yes," Uncle says. "This is a very good thing. It means we have some time to find our way back before midnight."

"A few days…" Mom trails off. "So, it has only been a few…seconds in your world since you've been back here?"

"Huh, yeah, I suppose it has," I say. "I'm going back out to the tree. It called to me so many times before, maybe it will again."

I stand in front of the large oak as I breathe in the air around me. I try to clear myself of all thoughts as I take in the feeling of magic drumming rapidly through me. If I stand perfectly still and really concentrate, I can feel Vincent near me, as if he is standing directly in front of me on another side of a veil I can't see. And then it hits me. It has to be a type of veil that connects the worlds. One that can't be seen but is always there. But how do I access it? How do I open a veil to another world? I reach out my hand, and I swear I can feel Vincent's touch. The comforting vibration washes over me, and I fall to my knees.

I'm still on my knees as the sun sets around me. I've been out here for hours, failing in all attempts to open a doorway to my world. I'm a goddess, but how much of a goddess can I be if I can't even travel between worlds?

"Thaddeus, Valentina, can you hear me?" I say aloud. I wait for a long moment, listening for their voices. I remember them so well from the vision I had; I would know if they called out to me.

When I don't get a response, I feel utterly ridiculous. Did I really think two people who have been dead for centuries could just show up in front of me and tell me exactly what to do?

Well, one could hope.

"Ren, why don't you come inside? You've been out here all evening." Mom says as she sits down next to me.

"I can feel him, Mom. He's right there," I point in front of me. "He's there, but there's a whole world blocking my view. I just have to figure out how to open it."

"You will," she says, matter-of-factly. "I have no doubt that you will. I think after a good night's rest, you'll have the answers you need."

"How do you know?" I say, looking at her now.

She shrugs her shoulders as she thinks for a moment. "I just do. Just like I knew you'd find your way to Vincent the first time."

"Are you sure you're human?" I ask. "I mean, are you sure you don't possess magic? You know too much not to."

"Honestly, I'm not sure of anything anymore." She pauses for a moment, looking toward my imaginary veil as she contemplates something. "One thing I do know is, your world is calling to me too. I can feel it, stronger now than I could before. My veins feel like they're vibrating."

My eyes grow wide as I look into hers. "That's the exact feeling I have with Vincent."

"I know," she says with a smile. "And I feel it too, but in a different way, if that makes sense."

"No, but not much does, so that's okay," I say.

She chuckles as she wraps her arm around me. "I wonder what it means?"

"There's only one way to find out," I say. "Come with me."

"Can I do that?" She asks excitedly.

"I don't see why not. You're connected to it too. Somehow, some way, you are. I think you belong there just as I do."

She lets out a peaceful sigh as she looks at the tree in front of us. "I think I do."

Chapter 29

I'm walking along a small pathway leading deep into the forest of Alba. The moss brushes softly beneath my feet as I near the tree where it all began. In front of me, there are two figures. They aren't human, though. They're far more stunning than any being I've ever seen. An overwhelming sense of peace and love warms my body as I draw closer. The emotions are so intense that I feel I could break down and cry from the sheer beauty of it all. But I hold myself together and remain strong as I finally make my way to the two beings. Their beauty stuns me into silence. They glow in a shade of angelic white, hovering just slightly above the ground. I can't see their faces; they don't even seem to have any. Just two glowing figures, resembling the shape of humans.

"Serenity," one of the beings says. I immediately recognize the voice and let out a small gasp.

"Valentina," I say. "You did hear me."

"We heard you, my child. It was such a pleasant surprise we never expected. We didn't know you even knew about us," she says.

"I…I just found out," is all I can manage to say.

"And we just found out about all that you and Vincent have been through," Thaddeus chimes in. "We're sorry we couldn't have been there for you before now."

"You see," Valentina begins, "it wasn't until you called to us that our souls woke once more."

"So, you've been dead, dead for this long?" I ask, stunned. They're a god and goddess. I never thought it possible that they could just cease to exist, even in death.

Thaddeus laughs. "Not in the way you're thinking, my dear. In our death, we have been two souls together all this time, but there was a problem when we created you."

My heart begins to pound rapidly in my chest, and I'm convinced they can hear it, for they draw closer to soothe me.

"The part of us that made us remember life was lost to us once we created you. It was much more powerful than I ever anticipated. It took a large amount of our energy in creating you. It wasn't until you called out to us that we remembered once more," Valentina says.

"Huh," I say with a nervous laugh. "So, you're my…my parents?" I ask. Saying it out loud sounds absurd and childish, but what else is there to say? But if they are my parents that means… Vincent…

"No," I say in a stern voice. "No, that would mean Vincent is my…my…" I can't get the words out, for I might vomit in front of the god of peace and the goddess of love.

"No, no, my child. We are not your parents as you call it," Valentina says in a soothing voice.

I almost melt with relief. Thank the gods. I don't know how I never thought of it before, but I couldn't even fathom the thought of Vincent and I being…related.

"We created you, yes. But you are not of our flesh or of our blood," Valentina continues.

"But the ceremony you performed. You had to be…uh…intimate," I stutter. Isn't that how any life is created?

Valentina nods, "yes, but it was because we were creating the greatest force to exist, love itself. In order to create love, we had to perform the ceremony out of love."

"And what better way to show your love?" Thaddeus adds.

I let out a sigh of relief as I look between the two of them. My creators. And I feel an immense love for both as if I had known them my entire life. I suppose in a way, I have.

"What do I do now? How do I get back to Vincent?" I ask.

"You already know the way. Listen to your soul and it will guide you back to him," Valentina says.

"I've tried that! I tried for hours, and nothing happened. I could feel him, but I couldn't reach him."

"Look closer," she says.

It's in that moment that I feel him stronger than I have before. As I look up, he is standing directly in front of me, his expression full of relief and an immense amount of love.

"Ren," he says, his voice cracking with emotion.

"Vincent," I say as I reach for him. But our hands go through each other as if we're ghosts. I look over to Thaddeus and Valentina, desperate for them to let me touch him, even just once.

"Neither of you are here, my darlings. This is but a vision. Your hearts and your minds are here with us, but your souls are not. You are only seeing each other now to find the strength you need to find your way back to one another," Valentina says.

"Where are you?" I ask Vincent.

"I haven't left the tree of Alba since you disappeared. I haven't had the strength," he says.

My heart breaks, for I know exactly how he is feeling. I don't have the strength either.

"I'm by a tree too, very similar to the one at the Isle of Alba," I say.

Thaddeus looks to me now. "Once you wake, go to the tree. Both of you. You'll know what to do then."

I nod and look back over to Vincent. "I will find you again. I will always find my way back to you."

"I'll be right here waiting for you. I won't leave this place until you're back in my arms once more," he says.

My soul aches for him worse than ever, and even in this dream state, I can feel it trying to rip closer to him.

"Wake now, our children. Wake and find one another. The time is upon you to do what you have always been destined for," Valentina says.

"We will be seeing you soon," Thaddeus adds.

Before I get a chance to say goodbye, they're gone. And I can feel myself drifting back to consciousness.

Chapter 30

I awaken to the sound of hushed voices, strained and full of emotion. It takes only a moment for me to realize what's happening. Sheila. She is here and arguing quietly with my mother. My oldest friend from this realm. The one who made me feel as though I was going insane when I tried confiding in her about my dreams. She shut me down without a second thought, telling me I needed help. In a way, I couldn't blame her. But it was the way she went about it. She never heard what I had to say. She never truly listened to me. She only accused me of being crazy and needing help.

I draw closer to the doorway, trying to hear what she has to say.

"You cannot be serious, ---. Do you know how ridiculous this sounds?"

My mom lets out a frustrated huff. "I know how it sounds, Sheila. But I'm telling you it's true."

"I confided in you about Ren so you could get her help, not so you could follow in the same delusion as her," she spews.

Her last words cut through me with a hot rage. Not only was she calling me crazy, she is now targeting my mother.

"You will not speak to my mother that way, Sheila," I say as I emerge from the bedroom and into the kitchen where they are standing.

Sheila pauses, her mouth gaping slightly as she looks me over. I know I must look different, for I feel different. The power surging through me now as Vincent and I are so close to merging our souls must show immensely within me.

"Ren…" She trails off.

"Sheila," I say in a threatening voice. Looking at her now, I no longer feel the bond I once had with her. It is now replaced with anger.

"I...where have you been?" She stutters over her words.

I draw closer to her, not taking my eyes from hers, and she takes a step back. "I've been exactly where my mother told you I was. I've been in my own realm. The one you never believed existed. With the man you never believed existed."

Sheila looks between my mother and me, her own anger forming across her face. "How can you…?" She trails off as Uncle Edmond walks into the kitchen. "Who is this?" She asks.

"My uncle," I say, still not taking my gaze from her.

"You don't have an uncle," she says in a huff. "Remember, I've known you our whole lives, Ren. Is this the man you claim to dream about? The one who has turned you into this…this person I no longer recognize? What happened? Did you run off with him this whole time? Is that where you've been?"

My blood begins stirring to a steady boil as she speaks. Belittling me, my mother, and now my uncle? I try ignoring the feelings of anger bubbling to the surface, for I don't have time for any of this. I must get back to Vincent before it's too late.

I turn away from her to face Uncle Edmond. "Valentina and Thaddeus came to me last night. They told me how to proceed. We need to get to the tree immediately."

"The tree?" Sheila huffs. "The one you're convinced holds the key to all of life's mysteries?"

I stay silent as I glare at her. It's taking every bit of strength I have not to allow my magic to come to the surface.

In my silence, she now draws closer, prodding into my ever-growing nerves further. "Well then, *goddess*, show me. Why don't you show us all how your voodoo works?"

No matter how hard I try now, my anger cannot be held back. Nor do I care. The magic welling inside of me picks up as wind rushes around me, threatening to destroy everything in this room as the cupboards fly open. Dishes shatter loudly across the floor as they come flying out. Sheila jumps, a loud gasp escaping her lips as she stares at me in horror. "What the hell was that?" She asks, her voice cracked.

"My voodoo as you like to call it," I say. The wind is still whirling viciously around me as I stalk closer to her. With a quick flick of my wrist, I throw her against the counter, my magic doing all the work to hold her still as she tries desperately to wiggle free.

"Ren!" She says in a pleading, nervous voice. Her nervousness quickly turns to realization as her eyes widen. "Ren…" she says in awe. "It's true, isn't it? It's…all of it is true."

"As I've said," I say, my voice calming slightly. I should feel bad for this. For all of it. It's not her fault for not believing in such things. In this realm, magic, goddesses, all of it, is nothing but works of fiction. It has never been a possibility here. I could have remained patient with her as I calmly showed her my world and my abilities. It would have prevented any of this from happening. And maybe at a different time it could have been that way. But now, with all that is happening, being torn away from Vincent and thrown into this world for a second time as we neared the last hours of performing our ceremony, has tested my patience to limits I didn't know were possible.

Finally, I reign my magic in, letting Sheila go. She gasps slightly as if she had been holding her breath this whole time. Which, truthfully, she probably was. I glance over at my mother for the first time since I used my magic in anger, and she's watching me intently. It wasn't fear in her eyes, not in the slightest. She was awestruck. She had always known that there was something about me and believed me faithfully when I told her about Vincent, even helping me find my way back to him. And she believed me still when I came back, informing her I was a goddess. But she had never seen my magic before.

"It's time we go," I say as I turn to head for the back door, leading to the fateful tree that would hopefully, once again, lead me back to Vincent.

And gods help me, it would be for the very last time.

My mother and Uncle Edmond follow quickly behind me as I make my way outside, the sun barely peeking over the trees, though morning had been here for hours. It's autumn here, with the winter solstice quickly approaching. The daylight hours are shorter as night grows longer. And though all leaves had long since fallen from its branches, the large oak standing in the middle of the field remained untouched, unbothered by mother nature. Her branches are still bright and full as if summer had just arrived. I never noticed before how peculiar that really was. But now, knowing all that I do, this very tree is a part of me, of who I am.

"Ren," Sheila says as she runs up to me. I give her a sideways glance as I keep walking, not bothering to stop for more conversation.

"Ren, please. I'm sorry. You must see how this all looked to me," she pleads.

I stop now, just feet away from the oak as I look at her, my eyes softening. "I do know," I say as I let out a long sigh. "Sheila, I'm sorry. Truly, I am. I do not ever use my magic in a bad or harmful way to those who are innocent. And I'm sorry you had to see that side of me. But there are things happening now, things so dire in nature that I just did not have the patience for the way you were talking to us," I say.

"I never meant to. This is all just so bizarre to me. And if I'm being honest, I always knew something was different about you, even when we were kids. Something special. I just refused to let myself believe in such things," she says as she kneels before me. "I'm asking you, as my goddess, to please forgive me."

I gently grab her arm and pull her up. "Please don't ever kneel to me. Of course, I forgive you," I say. She wraps me in a tight hug and gently sobs into my shoulder.

"Can I come with you?" She asks in a small voice.

I give her a soft smile and shake my head. "No, Sheil. I'm sorry. You don't belong in my realm. And with all that is happening, it's far too dangerous for a mortal. I won't see you in any danger."

"Will I ever see you again?"

"I'll make sure of it," I promise. "I'll visit you every chance I get. And who knows? Maybe someday I can even show you where I'm from."

"I'd like that," she says with a smile.

My mother walks up to me now and wraps me in a tight hug as tears slide fiercely down her cheek. "Make sure to visit your mother often, too," she says.

I pull her away from me just enough to look at her. "What makes you think I'm leaving you behind?" I ask.

She looks at me stunned. "But I thought it wasn't safe for..." She trails off, confused.

I shake my head, unsure myself. "Valentina and Thaddeus made sure to let me know that you must come with me. I'm not sure why. But they were insistent."

"They said that?" She asks, excitement growing in her tone.

"They didn't use words exactly. It was more of a lingering voice in my head as I woke," I say, shaking my head trying to make sense of it all. Saying things like this in a world so lacking in magic still makes me feel crazy.

She lets out an excited sigh. "Oh, I'm so excited!" She squeals.

"You might change your mind about that once you meet Celest in the flesh," I say. I pause, thinking intently. "Though, I get the feeling, somehow, you belong there, too."

She nods. "I know I do. I just don't know why or how."

"Shall we, then?" I say and gesture toward the tree.

In that instant, I feel not only excitement but also intense nervousness. What if I can't find my way back? As I stare up at the tall oak that stands before me, my heart begins to pound out of control. I know that somewhere here, in what looks like nothing more than a meadow, is a veil that will let me enter the world where I belong. And I know that just on the other side of that veil, Vincent is waiting for me.

I close my eyes, letting the power build as I feel it bubbling to life within me. But I fear it's not nearly enough to open the veil between worlds. I let out a shaky breath as I reluctantly open my eyes and scan the area. Nothing.

"You can do this, Ren. I know you can," my mom says as she places a gentle hand on my arm.

I give a quick nod before focusing all my attention on the tree once more. I close my eyes again, picturing Thaddeus and Valentina. I call out to them in silence, asking for the knowledge I require to make this happen. It's as though they were already there waiting, for I feel that once-bubbling power turn into a massive surge through my veins. I then call to Vincent, not knowing exactly if it'll work in the same way as it did with Thaddeus and Valentina, for he is still living, in physical form, in another world.

And then I feel it.

The sudden familiar vibration of his presence pulsates against every inch of my skin in soothing waves. I let out a satisfied sigh as I take in the feeling of his soul dancing with mine, a sensation I've grown to adore. Crave, even.

The power I feel becomes more intense than ever with the four of us, two gods, and two goddesses, joined as one in this moment.

"Oh. My. God." I hear Sheila gasp from behind me. I open my eyes, the power of four massive entities still very much alive inside of me.

I quickly realize why Sheila gasped in amazement as I look around me. It's as though the world has stood completely still. The wind has stopped, even the birds have stopped singing. I hear no vehicles on the road out front, no laughter or people talking from neighboring houses as I usually do. Even the air seems unreal. I notice a faint glow around my entire body from the corner of my eye. As I look down at myself, I can't help but gasp too, for my entire being is glowing hot and white. I look over to my mother and Uncle Edmond as they stare at me, eyes wide with bewilderment.

"Now we may go," I say with confidence as I raise my hand in front of me.

The ground rumbles slightly as a crack begins to form seemingly from nowhere directly in front of us. Through the crack is the same white light my body currently still glows. Much like the orb when I first rediscovered who I was, it begins to grow just enough for a body to walk through.

I grab my mom's hand, gently squeezing to reassure her. With the power I now possess, I can feel her growing anxiety as if it were my own. But amidst it all, I also feel her excitement.

"Does it hurt?" she asks.

"Not a bit," I assure her. "If anything, it makes you feel more alive than ever before."

Uncle Edmond comes up to me now, putting a hand on my back as he smiles down at me. "Are you finally ready to see your Vincent again?"

My heart skips a beat as I feel my face flush. I respond by moving forward, the veil's power entwining with my own as I reach out to it. I can feel Vincent now, his presence so strong as if he were right next to me. I suppose in a way, he is. He is only one step away, yet worlds apart.

One step away, until my destiny begins once and for all.

Chapter 31

The journey back to my world is different from last time. Before, everything went black as unconsciousness dug its roots deep within me. Nothing made sense as uncertainty still clouded my mind from the curse. This time, though, the experience of stepping through the portal between worlds is one I'll never forget. Power surged through me as I reached my hand forward, desperate to finally reach my home once again. The familiar tingling became increasingly stronger as I felt Vincent's soul reaching for mine.

An almost unbearable pleasure reached my fingertips and found its way into my heart as I felt Vincent's hand beginning to grasp mine. I finally stepped all the way through the portal and fell into his arms. The warmth of his body envelopes mine as I breathe him in. I've never felt more at peace than I do in this very moment. No matter what danger hangs in the balance, it doesn't matter. Not right now.

"I'm sorry," Vincent whispers against my ear.

"What are you sorry for?" I ask, not bothering to let him go long enough to look up at him.

"I told myself I would never let that happen again. That you would never be ripped from this world again. From me."

I finally pull away just enough to look into his eyes. I place my hand on his cheek as I give him a soft smile. "There was nothing either of us could do. But now, Vincent Atticus, now nothing can stop us. Not even Celest. Thaddeus and Valentina are with us," I say. And I know they are, for I can feel their lingering presence amongst us just as I had before stepping through the portal.

"I know," he whispers. "I can feel them, too."

I wrap my arms around his neck and kiss him deeply. The passion quickly reaches low in my belly as he puts a hand on the back of my neck, pulling me in closer.

"I'm never leaving you again, I promise," I say between kisses.

Vincent pulls away slightly as he searches my eyes, putting a gentle hand on my cheek. "Good," he says in a serious tone. "I don't think I could bear it a third time."

Reality slowly trickles back in as I realize we have an audience. I look over to my mother, who is watching us with loving eyes. "There's someone I'd like you to meet," I say to Vincent.

Mom slowly walks over to us, a bright smile beaming on her face. She doesn't say a word as she wraps Vincent in a warm hug. "I'm glad to finally meet the man who stole my daughter's heart," she says.

Vincent gives a warm smile as he glances between us. "I'm glad to meet you, too. And I'm glad you're here with us," he says.

"Here," she says as she looks around. "In a different dimension. In a different time." The look of shock settles onto her face as she takes in her surroundings. "It looks so different," she finally says.

"That's because this is the place of our creation. A place of magic," I say as I take in the same surroundings. It really is so different from the home she is used to. The trees have a faint glow as they hum with power. Even the small blades of grass and flowers along the stream have an undeniable power about them. Everything here is roaring with life in a way not at all possible in her realm. Even the air feels different as it wraps itself around all of us in a peaceful and loving manner.

"What is it that I'm feeling?" Mom asks as she glances around again. This time, she stops abruptly as her eyes land on my father. She sways slightly as a small gasp escapes her lips.

I study the two of them cautiously. Father appears just as shocked as my mother as he steps closer to her. And that's when I see it. The undeniable attraction between them that Vincent and I share with each other. And I can see something else too. I don't know how exactly, it must be a new power of perception, but I can see their magic soaring and entwining with one another as it dances in front of them.

"Mom," I say breathless from the shock. "You have magic."

"H-how?" she asks, barely glancing at me as she can't take her eyes from father.

"I don't know," I say in awe. How is it possible that someone from an entirely different dimension can possess the magic that we have?

"She's on her way here." Arian interrupts as she refers to Celest. Her tone is serious and panicked. I look over to her, her white eyes turning back to normal.

"How close?" Uncle Edmond asks.

"Very," Arian says. "We need to get this done. Now."

Redrich quickly appears, seemingly from nowhere as he swiftly leads us to the large oak. "We only have a few minutes until midnight. We must do this now," he says in an urgent tone.

As we approach the tree where it all began, I feel a rush of power like I've never felt before, not even with the four of us working together to get me back to my realm. It's different. It's all-powerful. It's mine. In that moment, I see two beings waiting for us at the base of the tree. I instantly know who they are, for I feel their strong familiar presence. But instead of glowing elegantly as I saw them in my dream, they're now in human form. Both so breathtakingly beautiful in the flesh, I can do nothing more than stop and stare at them in awe. Thaddeus and Valentina. So regal, an absolute picture of love as they stand side by side. I can see how they created beings as powerful as Vincent and I, for the love that radiates from them is unlike anything I've ever seen before. It's pure. It's raw. It's a love that surpasses all understanding.

But then I feel Vincent's hand in mine and quickly realize that the love we share, the love between our two souls, is easily stronger than that of any other. Even as I watch Thaddeus and Valentina, I can feel our love is the strongest and most powerful to have ever existed. Just as they had planned. My stomach flutters with excitement as I look over to Vincent, who is watching me with such an intensity, I feel my knees may give out.

Suddenly, the pain in my core intensifies, just as it had when Vincent and I first arrived at the City of Myria. I place my hand on his arm to stabilize myself before I collapse to the ground. The burst of energy felt between us only makes the pain worse. It is no longer the warm feeling I have grown to love. My vision blurs, the trees around us going in and out of focus so fast that it makes my stomach sick. Unable to handle it any longer, I drop to my knees. Vincent quickly kneels next to me as his head comes crashing onto my shoulder. I hang on to him as tightly as I can, hoping neither of us will lose consciousness.

My body feels as though it's being ripped to shreds as I let out a small scream. I notice Vincent has a fear in his eyes that I've never seen before, and I quickly follow his gaze. I soon realize why he looks so afraid. The small space between our bodies is filled with an intense glow. They dance around one another as they attempt to pull closer together.

"Oh, my god," I croak. The two light sources are coming directly from the core of our bodies. Our souls, no longer threatening to tear us apart to reach one another. Now, it is a demand. I knew it was only a matter of time before this would happen, but I didn't expect it to be minutes before the ceremony. We're so close now. We can't die before we've even had a chance for it all to begin.

"Somebody do something!" I hear mom cry. "Please, just do something!"

Valentina quickly reaches us, placing a hand on each of our shoulders. I touch my hand to hers, a soothing feeling quickly replacing the pain I felt only moments ago. She cradles Vincent and me in her arms now as she mumbles words I have never heard before.

"Even with the power I possess, I can't hold this off for long. Your souls are far too demanding and powerful, even for me," Valentina says. "This needs to be done. Now," she says as she looks over to Redrich.

She has a fear of her own as she looks at him pleadingly. It stuns me to see her in this state. The Goddess of love looking fearful has me nervous in a way I can't comprehend. Even with Celest close and trying to kill us before we can complete the ceremony, nothing compares to this feeling.

"It's alright, my child," Valentina says in a soothing tone as she senses my growing nerves. "I will not let anything happen to either one of you. You are far too precious."

She helps Vincent and me to our feet, and we stand pain-free, though the dizziness still lingers as it threatens to take me down once and for all. I can feel the body in which my soul resides quickly fading. And I know Vincent feels it too, for he's watching me with sad eyes as he places a hand on my cheek. I lean into it, letting the feeling of his skin against mine distract me from our eventual death if the ceremony isn't completed on time.

"It's past midnight," I hear Father say in a hushed tone. Which means if our souls don't tear us apart, Celest surely will.

"And Celest is almost here," Arian says.

Redrich reaches us as we stand under the large tree where it all began. Though big and powerful, it has a certain elegance to it as its branches gently hang low around us, creating a canopy. A canopy of power. A canopy of love and peace.

"Since the beginning of time itself, there has been a force so intense, so powerful, it has eluded the minds and hearts of many," Redrich begins. "It is something so incomprehensible that its true meaning has remained a mystery to us all throughout the centuries. Love. And with love, comes peace." I smile over at Thaddeus and Valentina as they clasp hands. "And though love and peace have been here since the beginning of all things, so has evil. It is a fine balance that keeps the universe in order. But as of late, the scales have tipped closer to darkness. It was during this time that the two most powerful entities, Valentina, the Goddess of Love, and Thaddeus, the God of Peace, made the decision, the ultimate sacrifice to ensure this evil would never win. They gave their mortal lives, and most of their power, to create a force even greater than themselves. And they are here with us today." Redrich stops momentarily to clear his throat from the tears threatening to choke him. "Though there is no name for what they truly are, I cannot think of a more appropriate time to give this great force a proper name."

Thaddeus and Valentina approach us now, our hands joined so we're forming a circle. They speak together in unison as though in this moment, they are one. "You are the embodiment of love and peace. You are devotion and passion. You are all-powerful. Though living in separate bodies, on this day, your souls will forever live in harmony as one. Through many centuries you have fought all odds set against you to be what you were always meant to be. In doing so, you have become Fate itself."

Fate. We are the God and Goddess of Fate. It feels so fitting with all we have been through to find our way to one another countless times. In this moment, as our name is given to us, a strong powerful surge enters our bodies. The dizziness quickly leaves as the fog begins to clear from my head.

"Fate," Redrich says with a smile as he approaches us. "As we stand here now in the presence of the God and Goddess of Fate, it is with pleasure that we witness the unification of these two souls."

Nothing more needs to be said as the ground beneath us shakes in rhythm with the power surging between us. The pain returns, only for a moment, as we witness the souls leaving our bodies, splitting in two, and then quickly returning to us. The halves of our souls that remain on the outside embrace each other only for a moment before Vincent's soul surges into me, fusing with what remains of mine. And I notice the same is happening to him. I also notice Celest in the background as she watches in horror. The scream coming from her lips pierces through all who stand before us. But her power is nothing compared to the power that is happening between Vincent and me. If it were any other time, Celest could have easily killed any of us here with the magic she attempts to throw at us. But this time, she doesn't stand a chance. With the ceremony near completion, our two souls now merged, the power that lies between us is far greater than anything she is capable of. And if it were any other time, I would be terrified in her presence. But now, all I can feel, and all I care about feeling, is the raw pleasure that bubbles to life within me as Vincent and I become one. The feeling captures my breath as I tilt my head back with a gasp, taking it all in.

Once our souls finish their merge, Vincent cups my face in his hands and puts his forehead to mine. I can feel him now in a way I never dreamed possible. It's as though every fiber of his being is now mine. Even our pulses match to the same heavy drum as we slowly catch our breath.

"Animae dimidium meae," I say in a whisper.

Half of my soul. The words come as though I have spoken them my entire life, when in fact, I never had. Not in this lifetime anyway. Quick flashes of past memories, past lives, come creeping back to me. Only I can't quite make out what any of them are or what they mean, but the language I spoke many centuries ago has returned to me as if I had never stopped.

"Amor omnia vincit," Vincent whispers back.

Love conquers all. How very fitting. For it is our love, our fate, that brought us together, and it is our love that will put an end to Celest, and anyone like her, once and for all.

I glance over at Thaddeus and Valentina, their once radiant essence now quickly fading as the magic within them dissipates. The residual energy hovers in the air for a brief moment before it flows into Vincent and me, merging with our own. As the magic enters us, I feel an overwhelming surge of energy coursing through my body. My senses heighten, and a profound connection to the world around me unfolds. The magic brings a sense of euphoria, as if I'm awakening to a new level of consciousness. I can feel their power intertwining with my own, amplifying my strengths and unlocking hidden potential. Despite the intensity, there is also a comforting warmth, a reassurance that Vincent and I are meant to wield this power together. The experience leaves us both invigorated and deeply united, ready to face whatever challenges lie ahead.

I take deep slow breaths in an attempt to calm the power that is now crashing through my veins. A tear slips down my cheek, my heart aching at the thought of no longer having Thaddeus and Valentina here with us. It was always known to them that once we were created and our souls merged, they would no longer be in the physical realm. But I know their souls will remain together in a blissful state of peace and love for eternity.

Their voices linger in the air briefly, their tone soothing, giving us the strength we need to move forward without them. Our creators.

Our love will always be with you, darlings. Though gone from the physical realm, our souls will remain by your side, our love and our peace guiding you in all you do.

As they disappear completely, their voices now a mere echo in our mind, our bodies glow a fierce, blinding white. Now with the ceremony near completion, I can feel even more than before. All my senses have kicked into overdrive, and it's as though I'm looking at the world through fresh eyes. The current I feel between Vincent and me has magnified tenfold. His touch would send me to my knees if I were without the power I now possess, for it almost does now.

And I can hear like never before. I can hear Celest panting like a rabid animal. I can hear my mother. To anyone else, she would appear to not be saying a word. But I can hear her silent pleas as she looks between us and the woman trying to end us.

I glance quickly over to Celest as she charges toward us. The anger raging through her in a manner that should scare me. But it doesn't. Not anymore. I know now, that even though I can't kill her…yet; we can stop her. We can slow her down until we can get us all away to safety. Just long enough for Vincent and me to finish the ceremony.

Finish the ceremony.

My heart flutters rapidly at the thought of it. We have shared our bodies in a way that seems impossible. Our souls tore their way out of our bodies to join themselves together. A process I won't soon forget. To most, it would be considered that we have shared our bodies in every way. And in a way, it is true. Though we have yet to share our bodies in a much more earthly and physical way. The way we've been wanting to since the very first time we met in the courtyard at Duix Castle. That feels like it was at least a few lifetimes ago. But now, it actually is time to share our bodies in a more physical way.

I can feel Vincent's eyes burning into me with a wild passion, for I know he knows exactly what I am thinking.

Let's get us all out of here. I need you now, more than ever.

It isn't words that Vincent speaks. I realize in this moment that we can share our thoughts with one another without a single word. My heart flutters again with anticipation.

I look over to him, the same burning passion in my eyes as we join hands. Everyone watches us, pleading silently. Something needs to be done quickly, for Celest is almost to us once more. If she were to get her hands on us, it would be all over. We're still vulnerable. And with my father's protection spell now expired, death is a real possibility for both of us. Vincent senses my thoughts, and I can feel the wrath burning deeply inside of him, igniting my own. Before, we wouldn't have a clue how to fight Celest. But now, there is no question. The knowledge we have now, the power, is like a second nature. Something that has always resided within us, watching and waiting until it could finally be released.

We move as one as we reach a hand up toward her, pushing the raw power begging to be released directly at her. In an instant, she's gone. It's as though she was never there to begin with. No traces of her, no signs of her presence. Just gone.

"Wh-where did she go?" Arian breathes in disbelief.

"She's back in Duix for now," I say. How I know that I have no idea. I just do. There's no use in trying to explain something to someone that I don't understand myself.

"Oh...right. Of course," Arian says as though the answer should have been obvious to her to begin with.

"The two of you must be going. It's time for you to complete the ceremony. Celest won't be stopped for long. She's angrier than ever, which makes her more dangerous than she's ever been," Redrich says as he reaches us.

I nod, trying to hide the excitement from my family. I don't need them to know how thrilled I am to get Vincent in my bed. "What will you all do?" I ask, changing the subject. Though I can sense Vincent grinning next to me. No matter how powerful of a goddess I may be, I still have trouble holding back the grin that threatens to escape my lips.

"Don't you worry about us," Mom says as she and Father come over to us. "We'll all get along just fine while you're...away," she says, struggling with her words.

I can't help it now. The smirk escapes my lips.

"We'll all head back to the city of Myria. We'll be safe there while we wait for your return," Redrich says.

That puts my mind at ease some. I know how angry Celest is. I can feel her, even with her as far away from us as she is. I feel the rage building in her stronger than ever before. She won't sit still for long before she comes back for her revenge. This time, it won't be against me and Vincent, but everyone else that I love. The thought makes me nauseous.

Vincent gives my hand a reassuring squeeze, reducing my anxiety a fraction.

"We'll be back to you just as soon as we can," I say to them.

"Please take your time," Arian says. "We'll be okay. I can see when she's coming. We'll have time to act before she reaches us. If she even tries to."

I nod, knowing she's right. I do feel a little better knowing Arian will be there to alert them of any danger. A sneak attack won't be happening.

"Okay," I say with a deep breath. "Okay, I know you're right."

"Besides, once you begin with completing the ceremony, you won't want to be stopping anytime soon," Arian says teasingly.

"Arian!" I say in a scolding tone.

She lets out a giddy laugh while Father clears his throat uncomfortably and Uncle Edmond studies and kicks at the ground like it's the most intriguing thing in the world. Mom's face turns a shade of red as she holds back a giggle, and Redrich is downright amused with Arian as he attempts and fails miserably at holding back a smirk.

I can't help but smirk myself as I glance over to Vincent, who is watching me intently with passionate eyes. My breath catches in my chest as we study each other, not so subtly.

Vincent clears his throat, still not taking his eyes from me as he speaks to our crowd. “We’re leaving now.”

Chapter 32

He grabs my waist, placing a soft hand on my cheek. I instinctively close my eyes at his touch, letting the sensation wash over me. Within seconds, we are back at our cottage. It's finally just us. Alone, without any distractions. Something I have been craving for far too long—many lifetimes, in fact.

Now that we're alone, an insatiable hunger grows inside me, one that cannot be tamed. I stare deeply into Vincent's eyes as he softly traces my throat with his finger. My pulse races beneath his touch, my body pleading to be explored further. He kisses the pulsing in my throat, softly at first, savoring the growing excitement within me. His lips become wilder, more untamed, as he moves upward. A satisfied moan escapes from my mouth as I tilt my head back, needing more. His lips finally meet mine with intense urgency as he leans me against the wall, his body pressed tightly against mine. As if he weren't already close enough, he lets out a hungry growl as I grab his waist, pulling him tighter against me, teasing his hard bulge against my pelvis.

"Ren," Vincent sighs. "Do you feel it?"

Our souls. Now combined as one and placed in two separate bodies. I can feel him in every way possible. His emotions bleed through and filter into me. And what I'm feeling now takes my breath away.

"Yes," I whisper, unable to say anything more. I'm too overwhelmed with excitement. With love.

The emotions dancing between us now are the purest love and adoration I have ever felt. I have always known Vincent loves me. There was never a doubt from the first moment we laid eyes on each other how much we both adore one another. But this…this is something different entirely. I can actually feel his love for me, and he can feel my love for him. It's beating between us like a drum in perfect rhythm.

"Can you feel it?" I ask back.

He sighs as he puts one arm around my waist and a hand on my cheek, kissing me. "Yes," he says with his lips still to mine, our fast, shallow breaths mingling. "And it makes me want you even more."

I smile, tilting my head back to look into his eyes, a devilish grin playing on my lips. Now, with my newfound powers, all I have to do is think of the bedroom, and we're there. Vincent looks around, realizing where we are, then his gaze slowly returns to me, a smirk playing on his lips. He spins me around to unzip my dress, the heat of his mouth teasing my neck.

His finger gently traces my spine as the zipper slides further down, finally reaching my tailbone. He freezes for a moment, and I can feel his excitement growing to immeasurable lengths. Finally, he places both hands inside the opening of my dress, gently gripping both sides of my bare waist. His touch no longer feels like a jolt of electricity. Our souls no longer threaten to tear themselves away from our bodies to join one another. The feeling is now one of complete peace, a whispering, soothing breeze that envelops us both.

With his hands still around my waist, he holds me closer against him, my back pressed tightly against his torso. I can feel the rippling of muscles on his chest and smell the sweet scent of his body. His bulge now teases the lowest part of my back, sending me into a whirlwind of exotic pleasure. I can hardly stand it any longer. I need this man, and I need him now.

“Patience, love,” he whispers in my ear, teasing me more. He can sense my growing pleasure, and it only excites him further. Despite his teasing, I can feel his arousal as strongly as if it were my own. I’ll be damned if I wait a second longer.

“I have none,” I say unapologetically.

I spin around to face him, kissing him hard, losing myself completely in the feel of his mouth dancing passionately against mine. I’m so lost in the moment that I barely notice as he slips the dress from my shoulders, letting it fall to the floor. I am now completely exposed to him, and instead of feeling nervous like I always thought I would for my first time, I feel an arousal like I never have before. I want him to see me, and I need to feel his hands against my bare flesh.

And I need to feel his bare flesh against mine.

Reading each other's feelings has its perks. Vincent's hands instantly begin to explore my body. He traces his fingers from my jaw, working his way slowly down to my throat, and finally to my chest. He stops briefly at my breasts, teasing my nipples only for a moment before working his way farther down. With each trace of his fingers, the heat intensifies, leaving a trail of fire behind. I ache intensely with pleasure as he makes his way down my belly, reaching my pelvis. I tilt my head back, taking in every moment, and his lips instantly find my throat. I let out a soft moan in response. His touch is explosive, and I'm convinced he is actually the god of pleasure.

Before letting him continue, I rip off his shirt, exposing the chest I've been dying to see for so long. I trace my hands against each crevice of his perfectly chiseled muscles. I slowly make my way down to the button of his pants, making quick work of it as I let them fall to the floor. And now, he is completely exposed to me. I reach my way back up to his chest, feeling his now racing heart beating urgently against my hand. His hard erection is pressed tightly against my bare flesh, and I instinctively push myself closer to him, needing him in ways that most would consider sinful.

If this is what sin feels like, I'll be happy to dance in it for the rest of my existence.

Vincent lets out an excited, shaky sigh as I tease him against me. He grabs my waist, pushing me into him harder.

"Ren," he whispers. "I need to feel you. All of you." He lifts me so I'm straddling his waist, his erection teasing my opening.

"And I need to feel you inside of me," I whisper back with my lips pressed to his. "Right now. Please."

His tongue teases mine with urgency as hunger rises in us with such intensity that I hardly feel the ground quaking beneath us. For a brief moment, I wonder if it's normal or if Celest has finally found us and is making her way here to stop the completion of the ceremony. But all those thoughts are washed away when Vincent lays me down on the bed, his arm still wrapped around my waist.

I close my eyes, losing myself in the feel of his touch, his hands caressing in all the right places. He uses gentle fingers to tease me between my legs, moving in and out slowly. Just enough to make me rise up to him, my body pleading to be shared with his. But instead of giving in to my body's demands, his fingers continue to tease me as he presses passionate lips to my mouth.

I grab his erection now, his hard shaft filling my grip as I gently tease it against me and his ever-working fingers. A low growl escapes his lips onto mine. I kiss him harder, continuing the tease. This pesky god of Fate has no idea what his goddess is capable of. I grab his waist with my legs, quickly rolling him onto his back.

As they say in the other world, “the ball is in my court now.”

I straddle him, my weight bearing down on his erection as I gently grab his chin to look at me. His breath is fast, the excitement growing in him to extremes. His eyes meet mine with such intensity that I’m afraid I will melt away to nothing.

“I have run entirely out of patience, Sir Atticus,” I say breathlessly. “I will have you now.”

He gives me a devilish grin as he caresses my ear from cartilage to lobe with a teasing finger. “What are you waiting for?” he whispers in my ear.

My heart skips a beat at his words, and the aching in my core intensifies further. This torture, this beautiful torture, is almost more than I can handle now. I put my full weight on him as he enters me fully.

When I say the world stopped, it isn’t an exaggeration. Everything—from the light breeze coming through the window to the rustling of little critters scurrying around the forest floor—stands still. The small particles of dust floating in the air around us seem to have stopped completely. Even Vincent and I seem to have gone from feverish with passion to blissfully still as we hold on to one another in slow motion. Time has stopped. The universe has shifted. And what was once lost to me, what was once a mystery, is now entering my conscious mind like waves crashing ferociously against a cliff's edge.

Before I can comprehend much of what is coming to me, time abruptly begins again just as quickly as it stopped. The complete bliss and pleasure I feel with Vincent come rushing back with a force that takes my breath away. I tilt my head back with a moan as he grabs my hips with his strong hands, making our rhythm faster and stronger. His lips quickly meet my throat, kissing it with urgency. I tilt my head back down and crash my mouth to his, my arms wrapped tightly around his neck, fists in his hair as the ecstasy continues to rise.

Vincent spins us around so he's on top of me, his member never leaving me the whole time. His broad shoulders ripple with each thrust, driving me more insane with hunger. Just as I feel my climax peaking, he begins to thrust faster, nuzzling into my neck, sucking softly as I dig my nails into his back. We both let out a loud moan as I clench around him, my release finally coming like a bolt of lightning. Just as I release, he goes still, his member pulsing inside me. He finds his way back to my lips, kissing me softly. Our breaths come short and ragged as we try to regain our senses.

As I lay here in a state of bliss I've never felt before, Vincent's soft, yet rugged body molded so perfectly to mine, I know I'm right.

He really *is* the god of pleasure.

Chapter 33

Sleeping would prove to be difficult. Then again, as god and goddess of fate, sleeping didn't seem nearly as critical anymore now that the ceremony had been completed. What *is* critical though, is having Vincent. Having *all* of him. Normally, anyone would be completely worn out by now. The friction, the heat of our flesh as we explore each other further. Swollen, chapped lips from the never-ending hunger of needing more of one another. But that isn't the case for us. Not only are we all powerful gods meant to protect this world and the universe from harm and evil, we have found we're all powerful in the bedroom as well.

Hours had passed since we first completed the ceremony. And in those hours, through the many caresses, knowledge began to flood my mind in waves. Knowledge of this world and the many others throughout all of space and time. Questions I've always had about the universe, I now have the answers to. And instead of being overwhelmed, I feel peaceful. I have peace in knowing all threats that are out there and how to deal with them as they come up. Neither me nor Vincent have to worry about what may lie ahead, because we can see it at every turn. And with that knowledge, comes a great responsibility I feel ready for.

Had this knowledge come to me before we joined our souls, I would have been overwhelmed, almost grief stricken in the fact that we had this heavy burden to now carry. I never would have thought I could do it all. It didn't even seem possible for me to be a goddess. That itself was too much of a burden for me to barely comprehend. But now, that has all changed. We were quite literally made for this, and I have accepted that with my whole heart.

Vincent kisses my neck as he slowly works his way down to my chest. I smile to myself in a blissful state of contentment as I put a finger on his chin, making him look at me. A sly grin plays at his lips as he continues his god-like work on my body. I almost give in and close my eyes as I let his lips hypnotize me once more. But as painful as it is, I remain focused.

"We should get back to the castle," I say, trying to suppress a moan from escaping as he works his way down further.

"Five more minutes," he says as he goes even lower.

Stay focused. Stay focused. I repeat to myself as I arch my back, as if I could possibly get any closer to him.

"I am focused," he mumbles as he nibbles at my inner thigh. I let out a gasp of pleasure as he chuckles to himself, proud of his handy work.

This pesky god.

I quickly take over as I flip him on his back and straddle his waist. He sits up now, as he puts both hands on either side of my cheeks and rests his forehead on mine. I can feel his member teasing me and I feel the excitement growing within me once more.

"You really are a pesky god, you know that?" I say as I touch my lips to his, kissing him passionately.

"Yes, and you love it," he says.

"More than anything," I say as I try to stop myself from lowering myself on to him and fail miserably. "But we really do need to get back to the castle so we can finish this with Celest once and for all."

"Mhm," he mumbles in agreement against my lips as he puts his firm hands around my waist, helping to lower me on to him even further. I feel the full length of him entering me, making me let out a loud gasp. "But all of that can wait…five more minutes," he says now that I've completely lost all senses to him.

This pesky, pesky god.

The sun has fully ascended above the horizon by the time we finally dress, its golden rays casting long shadows across the room. With the blissful oblivion of the night behind us, a knot of anxiety twisted in my stomach once more. Vincent and I were no longer vulnerable to Celest's reign of terror—the ceremony had rendered us untouchable. Actually, she should be the one cowering in fear. Yet, my heart weighs heavy with worry for my family. Our newfound invincibility didn't mean Celest wouldn't strike at those I loved in a last, desperate attempt to shatter my heart before we could rid the world of her once and for all.

Because she knows it's coming.

"Ren, everything will be okay," Vincent murmurs, sensing my rising panic. His touch gentle as he cups my cheek, and I instinctively place my hand over his.

I nod quickly. "I know. We just need to get this over with, so we never have to think about that horrific woman again."

"And we will. Once she's gone, we—" Vincent's words are abruptly cut off as a wave of dread crashes over me, forcing a gasp from my lips. Clutching my stomach, I double over in pain. I feel the life drain completely from the one man who had always protected me.

My father.

"Vincent..." I cry, the word escaping in a broken whisper.

Vincent's eyes darken with a mix of rage and concern. "I felt it too," he says, his voice trembling with emotion.

I straighten, a burning fury igniting within me like never before. Despite all the atrocities Celest had committed, nothing compares to this. She has crossed the final line.

"We need to go," I command, my voice unrecognizable even to myself. "Now."

In the blink of an eye, we are at the castle. The first sound that meets my ears is my mother's heart-wrenching sobs, each cry piercing my soul. I look down to find my father lying lifeless at my feet, his face ashen, his eyes void of life.

"No," I breathe, falling to my knees beside him. I lift his head in my hands, pleading desperately. "Please. Please come back," I beg, gently shaking him as if I could rouse him from this eternal slumber. But he remain cold and still.

"What did she do?" Vincent demands, his tone harsh and unyielding as he turns to Redrich. He is beside me now, his arm a protective barrier around my shoulders.

Redrich shakes his head slowly, pity etched across his features. "It wasn't Celest," he says, placing a hand on my shoulder. "This was the price your father had to pay for the protection spell placed on you and Vincent. He knew the cost, but he accepted it. He knew this was necessary."

Stunned, I stare at him, my blood running cold. "Why didn't anyone tell me?" I say in a harsh tone, my words spit out like venom.

"He didn't want you to know," my uncle chimes in softly. "He knew you'd be too reluctant to go through with the ceremony if you knew the truth. This was too important. Everything had to go perfectly. It was your last chance to unite your souls. Your father couldn't let anything stand in the way of that, not even himself."

I shake my head, refusing to accept it. "No, I'm the goddess of Fate, for fuck's sake! I can bring him back!" I cry, lifting my father in my arms once more.

"Come on, Father, please. Wake up!" I plead. I had lost him for most of my life, only to finally get him back. I couldn't lose him now.

"It won't work, my darling," Redrich says, his voice barely audible.

"Why?" I demand, looking up at him with tear-filled eyes. My mother clutches my hand, her grip a silent reassurance.

Redrich hesitates, his eyes filled with sorrow. "Because it was the completion of the ceremony that took his life," he said vaguely.

And then it clicked. It happened after Vincent and I shared a night of love. My father died because of me. Because I...had sex. "Oh, my gods, no," I whisper, collapsing back onto the cold floor. "No," I repeat, firmer this time, unwilling to believe it. It was bad enough that he sacrificed himself for our protection. But to know his life ended as Vincent and I came together...

Bile rises in my throat as I clench my fists against my face.

"Ren, you mustn't blame yourself," uncle says softly. "He knew exactly what and when this would happen. He chose to do it anyway. This is not your fault."

I couldn't respond. The weight of my father's lifeless body next to me is unbearable, and I begin to sob uncontrollably. How could such a beautiful moment lead to such heartbreak? How was that fair? Hadn't I suffered enough?

Lost in my grief, I barely notice Arian as she storms through the door and kneels beside me. "Ren!" she calls.

She freezes when she sees my father, her own tears spilling over. But she quickly regains her composure. "Ren," she says softly, reaching out to me. "I had a vision."

"What kind of vision?" I ask, my tone flat. If it was about Celest, I didn't care. She would get what she deserved. She didn't concern me anymore, not as I sat beside my father's body.

"About your father," she says.

My head snaps up. "Tell me."

"Think," she urges, her voice trembling with excitement. "Have all your memories and knowledge returned?"

I scanned her eyes, confused. Of course, everything had returned to me. It all came flooding back when Vincent and I united. But how could that help now? Even Redrich said there was nothing I could do. The goddess of Fate, completely helpless.

Anger surged within me. If I couldn't bring back my own family, how could I be the goddess of anything? What power did I truly have?

"Arian, I don't understand…" I trail off, realization dawning.

My mother.

I turn to her, and she seems to understand at the same moment. With all the knowledge that had returned, this truth felt the most natural. So natural that I hadn't given it a second thought. Across all realms and lifetimes, she had always been my mother.

"Mom," I said, a tear rolling down my cheek.

She lets out a soft sob and hugs me tightly. I heard Redrich, my uncle, and Vincent talking excitedly among themselves.

"The realization came to us too. I just didn't even think..." Redrich trails off.

Vincent and my uncle agree. It had been so natural for all of us. She was my true mother, in every lifetime.

Celest had erased this truth from our memories, casting my mother out and pretending to be her. She had been a loving figure only to manipulate and use me. Celest's cruelty and deception had kept me from my destiny for far too long.

"I'm going to kill her myself," my mother declares, standing with a fierceness and power I had never seen before. Reflecting on our life in the other realm, she had always been quiet and nervous, much like me.

But now I understand why. Neither of us were ever meant to be in that realm. It explains why she was so irresistibly drawn to the orb when we passed through this last time. Her soul was guiding her home, to where she truly belonged.

"Wait!" Arian calls out as Mother heads for the door.

Mother stops and slowly turns around, a dawning realization settling into her expression. She looks at me, then at Father, and swiftly falls to her knees beside us, clutching my hand.

"What are you doing?" I ask, confusion etched across my face.

She smiles warmly and tightens her grip on my hand. "Just as you and Vincent share a soul, so do your father and I," she says, an excited gasp escaping her lips.

"You mean...you're like us?" I ask in amazement, glancing between her and Vincent.

She shakes her head. "No, darling. Not exactly. We do share a soul, in a much different way from you, of course. Our souls were never joined like yours and Vincent's. But we are soulmates in every sense of the word. Thaddeus and Valentina created you, but they chose us to carry you and give you life. Because of that, they had to choose two people who loved just as deeply as you and Vincent do. That's why they chose Jack and Helen..." She trails off, looking over to Vincent.

Vincent looks down, his hand instinctively reaching out to clasp mine. My heart sinks with the realization that his parents are dead, killed by Celest when he was just a boy in this lifetime. I feel the sadness seep through him and into me, and I want nothing more than to shield him from that pain.

"She didn't want them to ever find out what you were, Vincent," Mother says softly. "She thought killing them would send you far away, ensuring you two would never meet. She didn't know fate was on your side. I'm so sorry."

Vincent nods, his voice barely a whisper. "Thank you."

"But what does any of this have to do with why you're so excited?" I ask her.

Her smile brightens as she clasps my hand. "Vincent, don't let go of her hand. It will take all three of us for this," she instructs.

"For wh-" I begin to ask, but quickly realize what is happening. A surge of power flows through me in warm, soothing waves. The three of us glow with a radiant white light, filling the entire room. It's a type of magic I haven't used before, but I instinctively recognize it. Any adept sorcerer would know the feeling of healing magic.

A healing magic that only the other half of your soul and two powerful gods can obtain to raise the dead.

I glance at Mother. Her eyes are closed, her face tilted upwards, and a content smile graces her lips. The light emanating from her seems to pulse in harmony with her heartbeat, each beat resonating with an ancient, powerful energy.

I look down at Father. The stark paleness of his face begins to give way to a healthy flush, his features relaxing as the magic takes hold. A soft, almost imperceptible hum fills the air, like the whisper of a thousand souls singing in unison. The energy swirls around us, a tangible force that lifts the hair on my arms and sends shivers down my spine.

The sensation intensifies, the warmth spreading from my core to the tips of my fingers and toes. It's as if the very essence of life is flowing through us, knitting together the threads of fate that had been severed. The white light grows brighter, filling every corner of the room, erasing the shadows and leaving no space for darkness to hide.

I watch in awe as the magic dances around Father, tiny sparks of light sinking into his skin, infusing him with vitality. His chest, still moments before, begins to rise and fall with the shallow rhythm of breath. The sound of his heartbeat, faint but steady, reaches my ears, a symphony of life reborn.

An excited breath escapes me as I see his fingers twitch, the color returning to his lips. The swirling light around us forms intricate patterns, ancient symbols of protection and healing that glow with an ethereal beauty. I feel the connection between us, a bond forged by love and strengthened by our shared purpose.

In that moment, Father's eyes pop open, and he gasps, life flooding back into his body. The light around us dims, settling into a gentle glow that lingers in the air. He looks up at us, his eyes wide with wonder and gratitude, and a tear slips down my cheek as I realize we have truly brought him back.

Chapter 34

Father quickly sits up, his breath still ragged as he scans the room. Mother is by his side, hugging him fiercely and weeping into his shoulder.

"How did I come back?" He finally asks, his voice croaks as he tries to regain his senses.

"You're asking a god, a goddess, and the other half of your soul how we brought you back?" Mother teases as she still clings to him.

He lets out a happy chuckle as he now reaches over to me. I hug him tightly for a long moment, really taking in the feeling of having him back.

"Ren, forgive me. I didn't think I should tell you the cost of the protection spell. I didn't want to ruin any chances you had at becoming who you were always meant to be," he says.

I shake my head, a tear rolling down my cheek. "It's all okay now, father. And I do understand. I just don't think I can ever thank you enough for all the help you have given Vincent and I over the years."

"You don't need to thank me, my darling. You didn't ask for any of this to happen. Everything I did, it was out of the deep love I have for you, my daughter," he says as he strokes my cheek.

No matter how powerful I may be, no matter that I'm a goddess, in moments like this, I will always feel like the little girl I once was when it comes to my father. It's a feeling I savor and always will. It's a feeling I'm thankful for. I know no matter what happens in life, I have this man to bring out my inner child once more, making me feel safe and loved in a way only a father is capable of.

Vincent comes to him now, snapping me from my thoughts. He wraps his arms around father, hugging him tightly for a long moment. Being so in tune with each other, I can feel he loves my father as his own. And I can feel father's love for Vincent just as strongly. After all, in our first lifetime, we all spent a lot of time together, building the city and the very castle we stand in today. Together, we created a safe haven for all Mirgorists, a sanctuary from the outside world. A place to call our own. In all of our other lifetimes, we were killed at a young age by Celest, the morbid cycle repeating itself over and over until finally we reached this lifetime where Vincent lost his parents. He was never raised by his father. In a way, all Vincent has ever had is my father.

Vincent helps father to his feet now, his color now completely normal as if nothing happened at all. Father lets out a confused sigh as he stretches his back. "It's light out. I expected to die directly after the ceremony was completed," he says.

Arian chimes in now, because why wouldn't she? "Yeah, well none of us expected them to "complete" the ceremony for so many hours," she says with a giggle.

"Arian!" I gasp as everyone lets out a chuckle. Vincent wraps his arm around my waist, trying to regain his composure.

"Well!" She exclaims. "Think of it this way," she says now to my mother and father. "You got to spend a lot more time together than you anticipated."

Mother giggles as her face turns a bright shade of red. She looks at father the same way I look at Vincent when I've had thoughts of having him or *have* had him. It's in this moment, I know exactly how they spent their time together.

Father clears his throat. "Ah, yes, Arian. How right you are," he says she he puts an arm around my mother, kissing her forehead tenderly.

Thinking back on the many lives I've had. I can only remember them being together, very briefly in one. The first one. I was a small child and I remember my mother and father as king and queen of Duix. Life seemed relatively peaceful back then. Or so I thought.

The very next thing I remember is Celest.

She slithered her way into our lives like a serpent, spewing her venom into our minds as she molded us and our lives exactly the way she wanted for her own gain.

My mother has always given me life. Celest bringing back mother and father's memories just long enough for me to be conceived once more, only to rip them away again. And again. For eight hundred years. And just as my mother has always given me life, so has my father. Even in the other world where Celest cast us away. I never was a product of rape. It was only another sick game Celest decided to play. As if banishing us from our true home wasn't enough.

The thought of all she has done to our lives over the centuries brings my blood to a raging boil. Vincent senses it and he's quickly to me, his eyes piercing into mine with determination as he gently grabs my hand.

"Let's finish this," he says, his voice dangerous and unapologetic. Yet his eyes, soft and loving as they meet mine.

A shiver of excitement reaches my core. Not only to end this cycle of torment that has been cast upon my family for so long, but for Vincent. The way he looks at me will never cease to make me weak in the knees. Even with all the rage that is churning to a dangerous level, he somehow always manages to calm my storm just long enough to completely take my breath away.

Sensing my thoughts, a sly smile plays at his lips as he kisses my cheek, his touch, the feel of his breath, sending my excitement into overdrive. I do my best to ignore the feelings igniting within me, for I know we aren't alone.

Celest. We must kill Celest.

"Let's," I say, an excited smile playing at my lips.

This time, I really am ready for war. The fear of us dying no longer looms over my head.

Though, with the power that now lives within Vincent and I, it won't be much of a war. With any luck, we will end this quickly.

Chapter 35

We quickly reach Celest's castle in Duix. This is the first time I've been back since the day she tried having Vincent and uncle killed. The memory still so vivid and fresh in my mind, though it feels like a lifetime ago. Because in a sense, it was. The feeling I have being back here, after all my family has gone through, makes the hair on my arms stand at attention. The way Celest made my life a living hell for so long still resides within me, casting a shadow of grief and anger on my soul. Our soul. I know Vincent is feeling it too by the way he is now staring at the door to Celest's throne room. The anger in his eyes wells to a dangerous level, fueling my fire even more, my nerves residing completely.

It's time to end this.

I look up at Vincent, his tender gaze softening as our eyes meet. He cups my face gently in his hands as he kisses me deeply for one brief moment. "Are you ready?" He whispers against my lips.

"Yes," I whisper back, my lips still brushing teasingly against his. I savor the moment. His touch, his closeness giving me the strength I need to face her for the last time.

With just a thought, Vincent and I swing the doors open with such force, they crash hard against the wall, threatening to break at the hinges.

Celest is sitting on her throne, slumped down in a way I barely recognize, a look of bitterness and defeat crossing her expression. How pitiful she looks now. I used to think she was the most powerful sorceress to live, fearing her with every fiber of my being. She was sure that she would win, taking all my power as her own, becoming a goddess herself. The thought makes me chuckle.

Oh, how she has been humbled. Even Celest couldn't intervene with fate. With us.

"Celest," I say in a cheery tone as we stride up to her, our confidence growing with each step.

"Serenity," she says back in a bitter tone. Her eyes go from me to Vincent, scanning us both quickly. She tries to hide her fear as she sits a little straighter, a look of boredom on her expression.

But I can sense her fear. I can feel it as if it were my own, and I can hear the fast beating of her pulse as panic rises as we stand directly in front of her.

"You're here to kill me I presume," she says, trying to keep her voice from faltering.

Vincent and I glance at one another, a smile forming at our lips. For it's in this moment, we know exactly what needs to be done. Without saying a word, we nod at each other before turning back to

Celest. Her panic rises to extremes as she looks between us, waiting to hear her fate.

"We aren't going to kill you, Celest," Vincent says in a calm and even tone.

Celest's eyes widen as she glances at me next, for I think she knows what is to come.

"Death isn't nearly good enough for you," I say as I stride closer to her, my presence threatening her greatly as she cowers lower into her throne. "We shall give you something far worse than death."

Vincent stands next to me now, the power between us swirling around the room with force.

"You tried keeping us from our fate for too long," Vincent continues. "So now, we're giving you a fate all your own."

"Celest, we hereby banish you from this realm. You will no longer be the queen of anything," I say. "In fact, you'll have no power whatsoever, for we have stripped that from you."

A look of horror crosses her expression as she watches the black magic once residing in her soul come to the surface as it lingers in the air briefly. It's ugly and ominous as it hovers before her, showing exactly how evil she really was. Together, Vincent and I lift a hand to it and squeeze. The swirling black magic now cracks and flickers before fading completely. All that is left is a small pile of black ash on the floor. But that too, quickly fades away to nothing, leaving no trace of the evil that once was.

Celest lets out a scream. "No!" She cries, her voice cracked and pitiful as tears well in her eyes. "You can't do this to me!"

"It's already done," I say in an unapologetic tone.

"We banish you Celest, imposter queen of Duix to a realm without magic. You will live out your days in a place you know well," Vincent says with a wicked smile.

She begins to shake uncontrollably, for she knows exactly where she is being sent. It is the same place I was forced to spend twenty-eight years of my life. The same place my mother was forced to live. It's only fitting that she now be sent to the same hell that was forced upon us.

I crouch down in front of her and I can feel her rapid breath on my face. It has a familiar stench of fear and I reach up to touch her cheek as I speak to her in a soft tone. "There will come a day, Celest, where you will die of old age. Can you believe it?" I ask in an excited tone. For it wasn't too long ago she was immortal, and I was a scared young girl who wished death upon her more times than I can count. "You will cease to exist entirely. And not one person will miss you or think of you ever again."

She shakes her head as a tear slips down her cheek. "No," she says. "No, please."

"That's not even the best part," I say, completely ignoring her pleas. "You won't be going there with no memory of this life or of who you used to be like I was forced to do. No, I wouldn't do that to you. I'm letting you keep every single memory, so you know what you had and what you were. You will live out your days dwelling over the fact that it was all taken from you. That it was you, Celest, that made your own fate."

Before she can utter another word, Vincent and I place our hands on her shoulders, a silent signal between us. The ground beneath us trembles with an ancient energy, as if the earth itself is awakening from a long slumber. Cracks appear, glowing with a mystical light that pulses in rhythm with our heart-beats. Suddenly, a swirling portal bursts open in the air before us, its luminous tendrils reaching out with a life of their own.

The portal's shimmering surface reflects a world beyond, filled with the familiar landscapes I was once forced to call home. A gust of wind rushes past us, carrying the scent of unknown realms. The portal begins to absorb her, her eyes widening in shock and awe. With a gasp, her figure is swallowed by the radiant glow, disappearing from sight as the portal closes behind her with a final, resounding thud. The ground beneath us stills, leaving Vincent and me standing in the silence of a world forever changed.

The air around us seems to clear instantly with a refreshing glow. The evil that once loomed over this land now vanquished, never to be heard from again. There is no longer a dark force seeping into the realm, creating chaos and fear. It's as though our world has awakened once more, a feeling of love and peace washing over the land as it was intended by Thaddeus and Valentina all those years ago.

"You did it," mother says, her voice cracking with emotion.

I look over to see her and father standing there, along with Arain, uncle, and Redrich.

I go over to them, hugging them tightly. "This place belongs to you once more," I say, looking between them. "No one will take it from you again."

Mother looks around the room with love in her eyes. "Oh, how I've missed this place," she says in a breath.

"Shall we get the place back in order, my queen?" Father asks her as he places her hand in his, kissing it tenderly.

She lets out a breath at his touch, a feeling I know well with Vincent. "We shall," she says.

I can't help but watch them adoringly as they embrace one another after all these years. Time seems to stand still as their arms wrap around each other, their bodies fitting together perfectly as if they had never been apart. Though the years have kept them separated, the love between them remains unchanged, as powerful as ever. Their eyes meet, and I see the familiar spark of affection, a deep connection that transcends time and distance. Their love has endured, untouched by the cruel hands of time, still as strong and pure as it had always been.

They are, and forever will be, Mary and Edward, the King and Queen of Duix.

Chapter 36

I'm in the stables with Juniper, petting his soft coat as I put the saddle on. Rides with my beloved horse have been more frequent since banishing Celest all those months ago. Though I am a goddess who is destined to save the realms from evil looming in the shadows, I still find the time to do the things I love. No amount of evil in this realm or any other will stop me from living a carefree life as often as I possibly can.

It has been four months since Vincent and I banished Celest. The land has become almost unrecognizable in that time. Mother and father have continued their reign over Duix as if nothing happened at all, their people adoring them just as they adore their people. The inside of the castle was completely renovated, no traces of Celest linger within its walls. Being there now, it's like Celest never was there to begin with.

Uncle still commands the army of Duix. His skill remaining just as strong and unmatched as the day he became commanding officer so many centuries ago. And Arian has become one of the most powerful seers this realm has known. Redrich has worked closely with her since the end of Celest's reign, helping her to hone in on her abilities. Together, they rule over the city of Myria as Arian as his apprentice. Someday, she'll be as powerful as Redrich, and I have no doubt she will do great things as her power begins to grow.

As for Vincent and me, our first order of business to get the realm of Mirgora back to its natural state was to destroy any remaining dark forces that resided. And that all started with the City of Albitar, the place of black magic. The same place where the stake of Albitar was cultivated and used in our deaths during our first lifetime together. We burned the city to the ground, leaving nothing left to remember the evil that once was there. In its place, a lush, green forest sprouted from the ashes, giving new, vibrant life to a once ominous land.

"Going for a ride?" Vincent's soothing voice snaps me from my tranquil moment with Juniper as I look over to him. He's standing in the doorway of the stables, looking just as magnificent as always. My knees grow weak at the sight of him as he steps closer.

"I am..." I say, anticipation rising in my tone.

"Care for some company?" He asks. He has a hand leaning against the wall behind me as he hovers close, his breath playing at my lips. His sweet scent hanging in the air around me, making my stomach flutter in anticipation.

I can't help but to laugh as I know we are reciting word for word the first time we went for a ride together. How long ago that seems now. The fear of us being caught together, knowing Celest would more than likely have both of us killed, hovered like a dark cloud. But now, there was nothing in the world stopping us from being together.

"I would love some," I say as I reach my hand up around the nape of his neck, teasing my lips against his.

The raging fire between us growing to extremes, he puts a gentle hand on my cheek, and the other around my waist, drawing me in closer to him as he kisses me with such passion, I lose all senses of the world around me.

"Maybe we can ride straight home," he whispers in my ear, his teasing lips against my flesh, sending my need for him into overdrive.

I can feel his need for me becoming just as urgent and I instinctively pull him closer, feeling his growing member against my pelvis. He lets out a low growl as his lips crash into mine, the intensity of the moment becoming almost too much to bear.

"Right now," I say as I work my way down to his neck, the primal need for him growing to extremes.

I feel the familiar rush of time and space swirling around us, the sensation of being caught in a whirlwind of energy. As my surroundings come into focus, I find we're standing in the bedroom, the soft glow of candlelight casting dancing shadows on the walls. The rich scent of sandalwood fills the air, mingling with the faint aroma of fresh linens. My eyes lock onto Vincent, whose determined expression makes my heart race. A sly smile spreads across my lips as it dawns on me that Vincent had no intention of waiting for the ride back to our cabin. His impatience has gotten the better of him, and I can see the desire burning in his eyes, mirroring my own.

"Well then, what are you waiting for?" I tease as I look up at him, anticipation rising in my core as I wait for his next move. He gives me a playful, devilish grin as he pulls me into his arms, our bodies molding together with intense heat as his lips do their god-like work against mine.

This pesky, pesky god.

About the author

Megan was born and raised in upstate New York, where she continues to reside today. She has a deep passion for writing, often finding inspiration in the serene beauty of her surroundings. Megan is also dedicated to caring for her thriving farm, where she spends her days tending to the land and animals. Her beloved dogs are never far from her side, providing constant companionship and joy. In her spare time, she indulges in various crafting projects, letting her creativity flourish in every piece she makes.

Made in the USA
Middletown, DE
28 July 2024

57926729R00168